She saw Lyle's face tighten instantly

"I brought the children to England with me simply as a good deed to help your sister, not with any desire for reward," Jay said.

"No good deed should go completely unrewarded." Unexpectedly his eyes fired. Lyle took a swift step toward her and grasped her chin in the fingers of his one hand, and with the other he took her round the waist and pulled her toward him. His head bent above her, and then his lips pressed down hard upon her own.

A tremor ran through her body, and her mouth moved under his, softening in spite of herself with an instinctive response that she was totally unable to control. No matter that her reeling mind cried out at the folly of responding to Lyle Gaunt's kiss, her heart yearned to put a foot on the forbidden drawbridge between them....

Lightning Strikes Twice

Sue Peters

Harlequin Books

TORONTO • NEW YORK • LONDON
AMSTERDAM • PARIS • SYDNEY • HAMBURG
STOCKHOLM • ATHENS • TOKYO • MILAN

Original hardcover edition published in 1983
by Mills & Boon Limited

ISBN 0-373-02583-1

Harlequin Romance first edition November 1983

Printed in U.S.A.

CHAPTER ONE

'THE fire wouldn't have gained such a hold if I hadn't had to waste time rescuing you and the children!'

Even allowing for the fact that his newly acquired inheritance had just gone up in flames, nothing could excuse such a remark. It was diabolical, barbaric. And so was Lyle Gaunt, Jay condemned the speaker furiously.

'Propelling myself and the children downstairs and out of the kitchen door into a freezing farmyard hardly comes under such a dramatic heading as rescue!' she flashed back at him angrily. Unconsciously her fingers reached up to rub her shoulder, that still stung with the force of his grip when he shook her awake.

'Jay, wake up! The Hall's on fire! Jay!' Brutally he dragged her back from the depths of travel-weary slumber. 'Get up,' he commanded her urgently. 'The Hall's on fire!'

Even as her eyes blinked open, and stared uncomprehendingly up at the face that leaned over her bed, his hand left her shoulder and grasped the bed covers, and with a quick yank he pulled them clear of her recumbent form.

'Get up, I said!' He dropped the covers haphazardly over the end of the old-fashioned iron bedstead, and without waiting for her to obey him he bent and put both hands under her armpits, and lifted her bodily out of bed.

'Get some clothes on.' He stood her unceremoniously on her feet, and his glance raked over her skimpy off-the-shoulder shortie nightie, which was all that had been necessary in the heat of the Gulf countries, and her face flamed.

'It'd have been just the same if I'd gone to bed without one,' she fumed. The thought crossed her mind

5

that she had not heard her reluctant host knock on her door before he entered, but before she could put her indignation into words, he pivoted on his heel and pushed his way through the communicating door into the smaller room where the two children had been put to bed, and threw over his shoulder at Jay curtly,

'I'll roll the children in blankets, while you dress.'

He had to raise his voice and shout above the thunder, and the almost continuous hiss of lightning that split the sky like an evil snake, and made Jay realise how deeply asleep she must have been, not to have heard it before. Too deeply asleep to have heard Lyle knock on her door, even if he had bothered to do so, which was doubtful, she told herself disparagingly. The thunder growled to a momentary halt, and in the silence her ears caught an ominous crackling sound that made her spine tingle. The crackling did not die away, but went on and on, growing stronger, nearer. She used the next flash of lightning to help her to locate her clothes. Fully alert, and frightened now, she wriggled hastily into a pair of slacks and started to pull a sweater over her head as Lyle reappeared at the communicating door.

He must have used a gentler approach with the children, because Holly was still asleep, her diminutive five-year-old form softly cocooned in a fluffy blanket. Tim, enjoying two years seniority to his sister, was wide awake and coping awkwardly with his own blanket, his eyes wide and excited at this new experience of fleeing from a house on fire.

'Get as far away from the house as you can.' Jay was still tugging her sweater over the top of her slacks as Lyle pushed them outside the kitchen door, and dropped the sleeping youngster into her arms. 'Not that way!' Instinctively she turned to her left, and his hands gripped her shoulders again, both of them this time, and pointed her to face the other way. 'The barns aren't safe. The hay might ignite if the wind blows a spark into it. Head towards the windmill.' His pointing hand indicated the dark arms of the mill outlined against the night sky, and moving briskly at the behest of the cutting breeze. 'You'll be safe enough by the pool, the wind's blowing away from the mill.'

Safe enough from the fire, but inviting pneumonia, Jay thought shudderingly as the biting wind cut into her shrinking flesh, that for the last few months had become accustomed to desert heat.

'What about you?' Her voice rose as, instead of accompanying them Lyle turned back towards the kitchen door. 'You can't go back in there,' she cried shrilly. 'If it isn't safe for us, it's not safe for you, either!'

'I'm going to ring the fire brigade. The flames still seem to be confined to the old wing of the house, they haven't reached as far as this yet.'

But they were heading in this direction with terrifying speed, Jay saw with a shiver, driven by the keen wind that seemed as if it was biting into her very bones. And Lyle had delayed ringing for the fire brigade in order to first bring herself and the children to safety. And now he blamed her for the delay, and the smoking wreckage of what he called the old wing of Millpool Hall.

'The fire's under control now, Mr Gaunt.' An aeon of cold later, a bulky figure in waders and a helmet strode up to them. 'I reckon it'll be safe for you to take the lady and the little 'uns back inside, out of this wind, though I should sleep them downstairs for the rest of the night if I were you, in case the fire flares up again. You never know with these old buildings, they're tinder dry, and in this wind. . . .' The fireman pursed doubtful lips. 'We'll stick around until it gets daylight, for safety's sake, though the storm seems to have passed over now.' A smoke-grimed hand tipped the big helmet back, and its owner turned a lugubrious look at the clearing sky. 'It was a bit of rare bad luck, for lightning to strike the house,' he observed. 'You'd 'ave thought it'd strike the windmill first, being on higher ground,' he criticised the vagaries of the elements, 'but you never know with the weather, do you?' he grumbled, and added philosophically, 'still, they do say as lightning never strikes twice in the same place, if that's any consolation.'

It was of no consolation at all, in her present situation, Jay decided unhappily. It was bad enough that Lyle had refused to take responsibility for his niece and nephew when she had presented them to him the day before, without him openly regarding her arrival with them as a bad omen, and blaming their presence in his house for delaying him those vital few minutes that allowed the fire time to gain a hold, and do its worst.

'I'm not responsible for the elements,' she denied spiritedly when the fireman departed, and added with a shiver, 'I'm going to take Holly and Tim inside, out of this wind.'

'I'll make sure it's safe first.'

'The fireman said it's safe, it we remain downstairs,' Jay insisted. 'I'll put Holly on the settle in the kitchen, and Tim can curl up on the window seat.' The sleeping child was heavy in her arms, but not nearly so heavy as the responsibility for another woman's children, that for the first time since she had so lightheartedly agreed to escort the pair to England, and leave them in their uncle's charge at Millpool Hall, felt a burdensome weight on Jay's slight shoulders.

'I'll carry Holly back.' Did her exhaustion sound in her voice, or was Lyle merely afraid she might drop the child if her frozen feet slipped on the mud left by the recently departed storm? Jay wondered cynically, but she surrendered Holly into his arms nevertheless, too thankful to be released from the child's weight to argue.

'Stay in the kitchen. Don't be tempted to go back to your bedroom for anything. Anything at all,' Lyle warned her sternly as he lowered Holly gently on to the settle, the while his tone towards Jay held no gentleness, and the look he cast on her criticised her for insisting upon bringing the children indoors before he had made a personal check to verify the fireman's all-clear.

'The fireman said. . . .' she began defensively.

'Even firemen can be mistaken.'

'But you can't, I suppose?' Jay flashed, stung by the censure in his tone.

'I intend to make doubly sure.'

'Then go and make sure,' she dismissed him impatiently, and turned her back on him and began to tuck Tim's blanket more closely round him on the narrow window seat, aware that her hands were shaking, and for some reason she was suddenly unable to withstand the wintry stare that felt as cutting as the wind outside, and contrasted oddly with the warm amber-gold colour of Lyle's eyes.

'I'm going to remain here with the children.' With her back turned towards Lyle, it was easier to defy him, she realised thankfully, and added for good measure, 'When Beth and Andrew return to England, I want to have Holly and Tim in good shape to welcome their parents, and their new brother or sister, whichever it happens to be. I don't want to have to explain to Beth that they're both in hospital with pneumonia, through over-caution on your part,' she flung his criticism angrily back at him over her turned shoulder. 'They're accustomed to the heat of the Gulf, and a March wind in England can do untold damage if they're not careful until they're acclimatised.' Uneasily she wished she had broken their journey to buy the children thicker clothes.

'You'd find it even more difficult to explain away if the children were injured in a fire because of your own lack of caution,' Lyle growled, and Jay's head came up sharply, her face whitening.

'I don't . . .' she began sharply, but she spoke to empty air. Lyle was gone. With a quick, silent movement that caught Jay unawares, he spun on his heel and was out of the kitchen door even as she started to speak. Briefly the rich auburn of his hair outlined in the light streaming through the kitchen windows, and then the leaded panes showed only the shadowy emptiness of the kitchen garden, and the low wall beyond it that separated it from the farmyard. Through the cold darkness Jay heard the wicket gate plop shut as he went through it, and Lyle's voice spoke and another answered him, presumably one of the firemen, and then—silence. Even the ominous crackling had stopped, Jay realised, tensely listening. In its way, the silence was even more ominous than the sound, because it gave her uneasy thoughts full rein.

'Tim?' she questioned hopefully, but with the easy resilience of childhood, Tim had followed his small sister's example and was already sound asleep, and Jay was alone, and more lonely than she had ever felt in her life before.

'I'll take the children back to England with me.'

It had seemed such a simple solution at the time. Her lips twisted now with wry bitterness as she recalled her airy promise to the distraught Beth.

'Oh Jay, would you?' her friend exclaimed thankfully. 'Andrew's caught up in these oil negotiations, and I simply can't drag him away at this crucial stage.' The children's mother grasped at Jay's offer with alacrity. 'Why junior had to choose this time to make his appearance, I can't imagine,' she wailed distractedly. 'He's not due for another six weeks yet.'

'How d'you know it'll be a "he"?' Jay teased.

'It's *got* to be a boy, causing all this upset!'

If her friend's prophecy proved to be correct, the new arrival promised to be the image of his uncle, Jay told herself sourly. If Beth was unprepared for the early arrival of her third child, Jay was equally unprepared for her welcome, or lack of it, at Millpool Hall. Nothing Beth said about her brother warned Jay that she might expect anything other than a cordial reception.

'Lyle's always said I could send the children to him in an emergency,' Beth told her confidently. 'He's only just taken over at Millpool Hall, and I imagine he's still trying to sort out the running of the estate there, but just the same, I know he won't mind having Tim and Holly for a few weeks, until Andrew and I bring the baby back home.'

'You go off and have your baby, and leave Tim and Holly to me,' Jay ordered her airily. 'After we land in

London, I've got to cross the country to reach Chester, and home, so it won't be all that much out of my way to make a diversion to your brother's place. What's it like?' she enquired, more to divert her friend's mind from her present problems than out of any real interest in the unknown Lyle Gaunt's inheritance.

'I've never seen it. Neither had Lyle, until he took over,' Beth retorted crisply, and seeing Jay's look of surprise added, 'It's the old story. My father and Uncle Quintin were brothers. They both fell in love with the same girl, and my father won. Over the years both my parents tried to re-establish contact with my uncle, but the bitterness over his unhappy love affair had gone too deep, and he rejected every olive branch that was offered to him. He even refused to meet Lyle, although my brother was his heir. I suppose he was afraid Lyle might have inherited my mother's looks, and he couldn't bear to meet him, and risk resurrecting painful memories.'

'Did your uncle never marry?' Jay asked, registering the fact that Lyle Gaunt was his uncle's heir.

'Never.' Beth shook her head. 'It was Mother, or no one, for Uncle Quintin. He remained single, and by all accounts buried himself in the work of running the estate, and according to what Lyle told me on the telephone after he moved in at Millpool Hall a few weeks ago, Uncle Quintin had succeeded in building up a fine herd of pedigree cattle, which made it all the more of a pity that he wouldn't allow Lyle to go and see him, because he's knowledgeable about cattle.'

'Does your brother farm, as well?'

'He was groomed to take over the running of the Hall estate, when it became evident that Uncle Quintin didn't intend to marry,' Beth said practically. 'Fortunately an agricultural career accorded with Lyle's own inclinations, and when he left agricultural college he went as a manager on a large estate in the South, in order to gain experience.'

'Your brother may not care for his inheritance, now he's seen it,' Jay objected. 'He might prefer to sell it, and go back to his old job, rather than bother to pick up the reins of a place he knows nothing about.' And where disappointment had been allowed to fester into bitterness over so many wasted years, she thought privately, although she did not say so out loud.

'Not Lyle.' Beth shook her head decisively. 'Millpool Hall's in his blood. He's already in love with the place, from what he told me, even if he wasn't before, from the stories my father used to tell us about it when we were children. There've been Gaunts living there since fifteen hundred and something,' Beth said with cheerful vagueness, her interest more in the immediate future than in the past. 'And if the Hall estate's suffering from neglect since Uncle Quintin had his last stroke, Lyle will regard it as a challenge, to get it running smoothly again.'

Lyle Gaunt was not the kind of man to turn down a challenge, Jay thought sombrely, although evidently the challenge of coping with two lively children for an unspecified number of weeks was one that did not appeal to him, a reluctance he made unhesitatingly plain to her when she presented herself at the Hall and explained her errand to its new owner.

'It's pointless you bringing the children to me,' he told her bluntly. 'I can't possibly accommodate them. Or you,' he added, with unflattering frankness.

'I don't need accommodation at the Hall for myself.' In fact, the quicker she could remove herself from the place and its odious owner the better, Jay decided angrily, and wondered how it was that a brother and sister could have such totally different temperaments. Beth was so friendly and sweet-natured.

'You'll *have* to take the children,' she insisted. 'They're your responsibility, not mine.' Although Jay was of medium height herself, she had to tilt her head back to look up into Lyle's face. Her hair was a cloudy darkness about the fine bone etching of her mobile features, that were arresting rather than being merely pretty, and illuminated by a pair of dark-lashed violet eyes that held a look of rocklike determination as she faced the children's temporary, and seemingly unwilling, guardian.

'I can't possibly look after two young children,' he reiterated flatly. There was no hint of compromise in his face, or his voice. 'We're right in the middle of the lambing season, and at the busiest time of the year, and there's simply no one here to look after them.'

'The woman who took them into the kitchen with her just now looks to me to be quite capable,' Jay retorted with equal firmness. She had discharged her promise to Beth by bringing the children to Millpool Hall, and fond as she was of Tim and Holly, she had her own work to do, and had no intention, she told herself resolutely, of being imposed upon further by their autocratic relative. If Lyle had asked her to remain until he was able to make some alternative arrangements for them, she might have conceded a day or two to oblige him until the children were settled in, but they had gone happily enough with the woman he called Martha, so there was absolutely no need for her, Jay, to remain at the Hall a moment longer. 'I've honoured my promise to Beth to bring the children here. Now you must honour yours, to take them in,' she told him firmly.

'It's quite out of the question,' he refused flatly. 'Martha doesn't live in, she only comes on a daily basis. This is a bachelor establishment, and I'm frequently out at night.'

Which was another way of saying that the children would be left on their own in the house while he was out, and if any harm came to them as a consequence, by inference it would be Jay's fault if she insisted upon leaving them there. It was moral blackmail, she thought furiously.

'Out where?' she snapped. She had not seen any discos when they passed through the village. One church, a pub, and a huddle of cottages, and that appeared to be Millford. And if Lyle had to seek further afield for his pleasures after his day's work was done, surely he could manage to forgo them for a week or two, in order to oblige his sister? So although she knew it was none of her business, Jay asked him abruptly, 'Out where?'

'Out on the sheep walks, attending to the lambing ewes.' His gritty tone said it was *not* any of her business, but he was telling her anyway, and Jay flushed scarlet.

'Surely you can leave that task to one of your hands?' she snapped. 'And in any case, Beth told me your uncle bred pedigree cattle, she said nothing about sheep.' She had seen the herd of cattle from the taxi window, peacefully grazing on the rich pasture. Unexpectedly, they were Friesians. 'They should have been Jersey cows,' she remarked jokingly to Tim. 'They'd have matched the colour of the house better, then.' The herd's black and white colouring grated on her aesthetic senses, striking a jarring note against the warm honey-gold stone of the lovely old house that met her delighted eyes at the end of the long drive. Her delight vanished when she came face to face with its new owner. In colouring, he more nearly matched the house than did his cattle, but he grated on her even more than did his magpie-coloured herd.

'The farm's a mixed one.'

Not nearly so mixed as her own feelings, Jay realised with sudden dismay, and wished he would look away from her. His eyes seemed to draw her own, and hold them, like a magnet.

'They're the colour of dark honey.' The thought seeped into her mind, that seemed to be unaccountably inflicted with a kind of blanket paralysis, totally at variance with her accustomed keen alertness. The thought was followed by another, equally unhelpful.

'I wonder if Lyle's eyes ever warm in a smile, like Beth's?' The two were almost uncannily alike in looks, but there the resemblance ended, Jay decided. Beth's smile was frequent, and attractively friendly, inviting closeness. Lyle looked as if he rarely smiled, certainly he had not smiled at Jay since she met him, and his aloof manner rejected any hint of closeness even with his own small niece and nephew. Impatiently, Jay thrust aside

the intriguing question of what it would be like to be
close to Lyle Gaunt.

'The late lamented Uncle Quintin didn't miss
anything by refusing to meet his heir,' she told herself
critically. She liked Beth, but she certainly did not like
Beth's brother. So why should his look upset the
normally even beat of her pulse, and make it curiously
erratic, and her breathing the same? She took a deep
breath in an attempt to steady them both.

'It must be the change in climate from the Gulf.' She
tried to still the uneasy turmoil inside her, that
threatened to destroy her capacity for rational thinking
just when she needed it most. The cold of an early
English spring had not noticeably affected the children,
so there was no good reason why it should affect her,
either.

'I've met dozens of handsome sheiks while I've been
in the Gulf, and none of them had this effect on me.'
She tried to laugh away her unexpected reaction to the
new owner of Millpool Hall, but her humour failed
dismally. Lyle Gaunt was not an Arab sheik. He was a
man of the north, his tall, whipcord frame honed to
perfection by a harsher climate, and his lean face
tanned by wind and rain, as much as by the sun. The
Arabs were open-handed in their welcome and their
hospitality. Lyle defended his solitary way of life as if
he pulled up a drawbridge between them, Jay thought
caustically, and furiously silenced the small voice inside
her that wondered, tantalisingly,

'What would it be like, to cross that drawbridge, and
reach the man on the other side?'

Lyle Gaunt had impact. That, Jay reluctantly had to
admit. He was not a man you could ignore.

'You would either love him or hate him,' the small
voice persisted, and before she could prevent her mind
from forming the question, it flashed a question back.

'In which category does that leave me?'

'This is madness!' she told herself, aghast. 'I only met
the man half an hour ago, and we've been at
loggerheads ever since.' But there was no denying the

fact that Lyle Gaunt disturbed her. 'Which is all the more reason,' she told herself on a note of panic, 'why I must leave the children with him, and quit Millpool Hall with all possible speed.'

'The children can remain at the Hall only if you're prepared to remain with them.'

Jay stared at him, stunned. It was an impossible situation. Lyle Gaunt was impossible! It was as if he had read her thoughts, and instantly moved to circumvent any plan she might make to leave. But to remain at Millpool Hall, under Lyle's roof, seeing him every day, was exactly what she must not do. Dared not do, if her rapidly accelerating pulse was anything to go by. It hammered a warning in her throat and ears, robbing her of the ability to speak, so that she swallowed in silence on a throat that was suddenly as dry as the desert sands she had so recently left.

'It'll only be for a matter of three or four weeks at the most, until the spring rush is over, and the young stock are able to fend for themselves,' he pointed out impatiently.

'Tim and Holly can't fend for themselves, but you seem more concerned about the lambs than you are about your own flesh and blood,' she accused him hotly, and added for good measure, 'In any case, in three or four weeks Beth and Andrew will probably be back home, and able to take charge themselves, and it'll be too late then, your help won't be needed.' By which time, Jay thought wildly, it would be too late for herself as well. Too late to return to the carefree existence that, in spite of her classic beauty, and a career that took her much into the company of men, had so far left her own heart, if not those of her admirers, curiously untouched.

She had never visualised her own heart's awakening to be like this. She felt like a butterfly, newly struggled out of the safe, dormant world of its chrysalis, to find not the expected gentle warmth of the sunshine, but cold, and harsh winds, and the threat of impending storm. To no avail she longed to shrink back into the chrysalis, or failing that, to fly as fast and as far away as she could, away from Lyle Gaunt and his ancient home, but once the safe cocoon of the chrysalis was shed, there could be no re-entry, and the tender, untried wings of her heart fluttered in vain against the storm, trapped by a situation that was not of her own making.

'If it's your salary you're worried about, I'll pay you whatever rate you settled on with Beth.'

'Salary? Settled on?' What was the man talking about? Jay wondered bewilderedly. 'What on earth are you talking about?' she demanded out loud.

'You accepted Beth's terms when she hired you to look after the children,' he pointed out harshly. 'It's up to you, now, to carry out the job you were engaged for.'

'You think I'm a nursemaid? A children's nanny?' Angry enlightenment dawned on Jay, and she exploded furiously. 'Do I look like a nursemaid?' Without waiting for him to reply, she swept on, 'Beth didn't engage me, and I'm certainly not being paid to bring the children back to England with me.'

'Then how . . .?'

'I became friendly with your sister and her husband while I was working in the Gulf—*not* as a nanny,' she cut him short impatiently. 'When Beth ran into—er—difficulties,' she declined to enumerate the difficulties. Let him imagine them for himself, she told herself unhelpfully, 'I offered to bring the children back with me, in order to help her out.'

'Are you a member of Andrew's staff at the oil company?' he seemed determined to label her and put her into a neat little pigeonhole, Jay thought cuttingly.

'No, I'm not,' she denied shortly. 'If you must know, I was in the Gulf to sell stained glass windows to Arab sheiks.'

Her interested eyes had noticed the glow of stained glass in a side window of the house when she first arrived. The thought crossed her mind that before she left, she would ask Beth's brother if she might examine it more closely. It probably depicted the Gaunt coat of arms, although from the distance of the taxi window she could not be sure.

'It's probably a lion rampant,' she guessed now with a quirk of humour. The Hall's new owner had the creature's colouring, and from the evidence of their brief acquaintance, its savage nature as well, she decided balefully. Her bald statement met with a predictable response.

'Don't be facetious,' he snapped. Even before he spoke, she saw by the instant tightening of his face that he thought she was merely being sarcastic about her reason for being in the Gulf, using an outrageous explanation to point out to him that her business there was none of his.

'He can make of it what he pleases,' she told herself defiantly. She no longer cared what Lyle thought. For good measure she added out loud, 'I brought the children to England with me, simply as a good deed, to help your sister, not with any desire for reward.' She had certainly not expected to be rewarded with such hostility, she thought ruefully.

'No good deed should go completely unrewarded.' Unexpectedly his eyes fired, but not with a smile. She had no time to discover with what. He took a swift step towards her, and grasped her chin in the fingers of his one hand, and with the other he took her round the waist and pulled her towards him. His head bent above her. She had time to notice the deep, crisp waves in the dark auburn shock of his hair, and then his lips pressed down hard upon her own, and a shock of a different kind shivered through her.

'He thinks I'm being sarcastic about the stained glass windows,' she thought. And this was his way of punishing her. His lips were an angry hardness, claiming her own. His fingers were a steel clamp under her chin, imprisoning her. For endless seconds, sheer surprise kept her still, and then,

'No!'

A sensation like a high-voltage electric current vibrated through her as his lips touched her own. It roused her senses to vivid, pulsating life, and made her heart leap crazily, as if it tried to escape from her heaving breast. A tremor ran through her body, and her mouth moved under his, parting under the pressure of his lips, and softening in spite of herself with an instinctive response that she was totally unable to control, no matter that her reeling mind cried out at the folly of responding to Lyle Gaunt's kiss, her heart yearned to put a foot on to the forbidden drawbridge between them, even as he pulled away, and left her suspended over a dark and terrifying moat of uncertainty and near despair.

'No!'

Her hands came up to push against him, clawing at him in a frenzied bid to break the unbreakable magnetism that flowed from him, registering the fact that even as she pushed, her strength was of no avail against the sinewy strength of Lyle's arms that, as she began to struggle, unloosed their hold and put her away from him.

'Loose me.' Her voice came out as a ragged whisper, but for endless seconds longer his hands still gripped her, at arm's length from him. Did he sense that without his support, she would have fallen, her trembling limbs unable to support her? She swayed as she begged him,

'Loose me.'

Still his honey-gold stare bored down into her eyes, while his hands continued to hold up her fainting frame, probing their wide violet depths that turned dark with the turmoil of emotions she had not known she possessed, until in one moment of blinding revelation, Lyle Gaunt brought them to life, and uncaringly left her to cope with the consequences as best she could.

'The meal's ready on the table, Mr Lyle. Will you eat with Miss Baron and the children?'

Lyle dropped his hands from her shoulders and turned as Martha appeared at the kitchen door. 'I might as well,' he conceded, 'it'll save time.'

'You might at least *try* to appear welcoming, in front of your housekeeper!' Jay hissed at him furiously, and anger stiffened her trembling limbs, so that she was able to stand without Lyle's support, and answer in a more or less normal voice when she reached the table, and Martha said kindly,

'You must be ready for a nice cup of tea, after your long journey.'

'The tea's very welcome.' And so was the food, Jay discovered gratefully, and thought, 'It must have been hunger that made me so vulnerable. I should have been more in control of my own reactions, if only I'd eaten properly during the day.' Bitterly, now, she regretted neglecting her own meals in favour of looking after the children. 'I'll feel better after I've eaten,' she thought hopefully, and forced her aching throat to swallow food for which she had little appetite. The tea steadied her. It was hot, and strong, and she spooned sugar into her cup with a reckless hand.

'Eat up, now, and have your meal in peace. I'll look after the children for you.' Considerately, Martha took Jay's two charges under her own wing, but her wellmeaning action had the result, Jay realised uneasily, of leaving herself exposed to Lyle's glance every time he looked up from his plate, on the opposite side of the table.

'Ham?'

'Thank you.'

None of the cheerful camaraderie she might have expected from Beth's brother, just a cold, formal politeness that extended reluctant hospitality to an unwelcome guest. He cut her a generous plateful from the home-cured gammon, slid across the basket of wholemeal batches for her to help herself from their crisp warmth, and top them from the crock of pale butter, and the preserves that tasted richly as if they might be the housekeeper's own treasured recipe, and all the time Lyle's warmly coloured eyes sliced through her across the table, with no warmth in them for Jay. It seemed as if each time she looked up, her eyes clashed with his, as if they were attracted to them by a magnet, she thought desperately, and forced herself to glance round at her surroundings, anything rather than at

Lyle. In self-defence she sent her eyes to roam slowly round the confines of the beamed kitchen, looking at, but scarcely registering, its spartan furnishings.

'Mr Lyle's not had time yet to make any changes.' Martha intercepted her glance, misinterpreted the reason for it, and excused the lack of comfort the room offered before it could be criticised. 'Mr Quintin spent all his time outside on the estate, and so long as his meals were regular, he didn't bother with the house. He didn't entertain, so he kept the other rooms closed.'

'This is a bachelor establishment. . . .'

'Lyle's description just about sums it up,' Jay decided, and felt an unexpected flash of compassion for the Hall's late, unhappy owner. The room was functional, and completely devoid of any of the homely touches that would betray the presence of a mistress of the house. One large wheelback chair stood beside the big open range, its hard wooden seat begging for a bright, chintz-covered cushion. There was not even a rug on the quarry floor, only a row of dents on the brass fender surround in front of the fire, a leg's length away from the wheelback chair, to betray the fact that weary feet had once stretched towards the hearth, seeking such comfort as the blazing logs could offer, since no other form of welcome awaited in the house at the day's close.

'I wonder how soon there'll be another chair on the other side of the hearth from the wheelback, now that Lyle's inherited the hall?' Jay's heart gave a painful wrench as she tried to visualise the occupant of that other chair. Would she, perhaps, be small, and fair, and fluffy? Unconsciously she shook her head. The kittenish type would not make a good farmer's wife, even though the mistress of Millpool Hall would not need to do more than supervise the day-to-day running of the house; would probably have a resident housekeeper to do even that. Perhaps the other chair's occupant would be tall and queenly, a Diana striding the uplands, as capable as Lyle himself of running the estate?

Intuitively, Jay rejected that idea as well. Lyle was all man, and would not want a manly woman as his mate.

'He'll want a woman who glories in being a woman.' The small voice inside her spoke up boldly, and in spite of herself Jay listened, obliged to acknowledge the truth of what it said. 'He'll want a wife who's truly feminine, without being a clinging vine. Someone who can match him mentally, yet still enjoy being cherished. A woman who. . . .'

But Jay had heard enough. With all her heart she found herself envying the unknown woman, and hoped fervently she would not be subjected to meeting her while she remained at Millpool Hall. 'I couldn't bear to meet her, to know. . . .' She dared not allow herself to admit the reason she shrank from such a meeting.

'If you've finished your meal, Martha will show you where you and the children can sleep tonight.'

'Just for tonight,' Jay promised herself determinedly. And presumably tomorrow she and Lyle would start to argue all over again. And as she rose from the table to follow Martha, she knew with a feeling of dreadful inevitability that however fiercely she argued her cause on the morrow, Lyle would be bound to win.

'It's a good job I aired all the bedrooms before Mr Lyle moved in.' Martha volunteered as they mounted the stairs. 'I didn't know that Mr Lyle was single, so I got everything ready in the nursery as well, just in case, and it's a good job I did, as it turns out, though I didn't think so at the time,' she admitted candidly, and added, 'Bachelors seem to run in the Gaunt family.'

Words, only words, but with the sharpness of arrows to prick and wound.

'It's a wonder the name's survived, in that case,' Jay retorted lightly, using other words to cover the hurt.

'Oh, the Gaunts survive, they're doughty fighters.'

But they, too, must have their Achilles' heel, Jay thought, and wondered silently what Lyle's weakness might be, as Martha called out to the scampering Holly,

'Not that way, lovey. I said, go left at the top of the stairs.'

'Left's the hand you carry your teddy bear with,' Jay supplied automatically. 'Let Tim go first, and follow him,' she admonished, as brother and sister jockeyed to be the first to find their bedroom door.

'You're both first,' Martha declared with masterly diplomacy as she put her hand on the knob and opened a door to the left of the head of the stairs. 'Choose a bed each in the small room through there,' she shooed them both through a communicating door, 'then we'll see about giving you a quick wash, and get you into your pyjamas.'

'I left the cases downstairs,' Jay remembered, and turned back reluctantly towards the door. 'Perhaps Lyle will be gone when I go downstairs,' she hoped silently, and Martha said,

'Mr Lyle had Bob bring up your cases when you first arrived. They're in your room, all ready for you.'

She should have felt relieved that she did not have to return downstairs, and risk meeting Lyle again. Instead, furious anger boiled inside Jay as she learned of Lyle's high-handed action.

'All the time he was arguing with me, he'd already sent my own case upstairs along with those of the children,' she fumed. 'No matter what I said, he was determined that I should remain here to look after Tim and Holly!'

'They settle in well, don't they?' Martha broke across Jay's angry thoughts with an approving nod towards the small pair, who were already busily investigating their new quarters.

'They're seasoned travellers.' Somehow Jay forced her voice to sound normal. 'They're used to strange accommodation. The only time Holly makes a fuss is if she misplaces her teddy bear. She won't go to sleep without him.'

'I'll help you put them to bed, and then I'll be on my way,' Martha offered helpfully.

'Are we keeping you? I'd forgotten you don't live in.' Jay spoke with sudden remorse for her own forget-fulness.

'There's plenty of time,' Martha answered comfortably. 'I get a lift in with the milk lorry in the mornings, but Mr Lyle always runs me back to the village in the evening, after he's finished the milking.' The housekeeper reached out and drew Holly on to her lap. 'I used to live in, when Mr Quintin was alive, but of course there was another couple here as well, then, the cowman and his wife, but they retired when the old man died, and it wouldn't be right, would it, for me to stay here with just Mr Lyle in the house?' she asked briskly, and Jay bit back a smile as she viewed Martha's white-topped head and ample form. 'Mr Lyle agreed it wouldn't be right,' Martha continued unaware, 'so I come in every day now.'

Jay's desire to smile vanished. Lyle had agreed for the sake of convention that it would not be right for Martha to remain overnight at the Hall, in spite of the obvious disparity in their ages and situations, but he had no compunction—none at all, she thought furiously—in making absolutely certain that she herself had no opportunity to leave!

CHAPTER TWO

'WHY aren't we in bed? What's that funny smell?' The blanket that covered Holly heaved and fell back, and the movement shook Jay from out of her reverie.

'What's that . . .' the small voice persisted plaintively.

'It's only the smell of burned wood,' Jay answered her as casually as she could, knowing from past experience that it was of no use trying to prevaricate with Holly. The fair-haired, blue-eyed innocence of five years old hid the tenacity of a bull terrier when it came to finding out something she wanted to know, and it proved quicker and easier in the long run to tell the small questioner the truth, as simply as possible.

'Is it still burning?' Quick interest lit the round blue eyes, and Jay knew resignedly it would be pointless to attempt to settle the little girl to sleep again until she had satisfied her curiosity.

'No, the firemen came and put it out. They've gone back home now,' she neatly circumvented the next question. The firemen *had* gone, her ears had registered the departure of the engine before Holly awoke, even though her mind was miles away.

'They've left the smell behind,' Holly observed discontentedly. The acrid smell of charred wood and scorched stone clung with the persistence of fog after saturation from the firemen's hoses, until it tainted the dawn air with an odour so strong that it was almost a taste.

'It'll go as soon as it gets daylight,' Jay soothed. It was almost daylight now, she saw. The kitchen window was a square of rapidly lightening grey, that when Lyle left her had been a square of black, pierced only by the lamplight from within that was already beginning to lose its strength in the competition from the growing light outside.

25

'I can't find my teddy!'

Jay's heart sank. 'We'll go upstairs and fetch him when we get dressed,' she promised, with a brightness she was far from feeling.

'I want him now.' The small face framed by the blanket puckered ominously. 'He'll be frightened by the smell.'

Which meant that Holly herself was frightened, and needed her teddy bear for comfort.

'I'll go and get him for you now,' Jay promised hastily. On top of an exhausting journey the day before, a verbal battle with Lyle when she arrived, and which bade fair to continue the moment they came together again, Jay prophesied uneasily, and then being rudely awakened by fire in the small hours of the morning, the last thing she felt capable of coping with now was a scene with Holly.

'Stay here and be good until I come back, I'll only be gone for a minute or two.' She bent and tucked the blanket firmly back round the small form. 'Don't move, or I won't bring your teddy for you.' A quick glance told her that Tim was still soundly asleep, and she knew that her threat was sufficient to keep Holly glued to her seat until she returned.

'Where on earth . . .?' The children's room looked as if a bomb had hit it, she thought with dismay. In his haste to get the small occupants out, Lyle had pulled blankets from the beds with scant regard for the rest of the bedclothes, which lay scattered with the pillows haphazardly across the floor. And somewhere under which, presumably, lay the missing teddy bear. But where? Hastily Jay bent to pick up the nearest sheet.

'Got you, at last!' she breathed triumphantly. It seemed as if she must have shaken out and folded the entire coverings of the two beds before she espied a fluffy yellow leg sticking out from under the final sheet. 'At least Holly hasn't started to scream yet,' she muttered thankfully, her ears straining for sounds of a preliminary wail from downstairs. Swiftly she turned towards the communicating door.

'Have you taken leave of your senses? What do you mean by leaving the children on their own downstairs? I told you not to go back to your bedroom for anything at all!' Lyle shouted at her furiously. He glanced down at her from the communicating doorway between the two rooms, and his eyes glowed with anger.

'They're almost luminous,' Jay thought dazedly. Luminous with anger against herself.

'Of all the irresponsible things to do. . . .'

'You're the last person who should accuse me of irresponsible behaviour,' she flared angrily, stung out of her shocked silence by his unexpected attack.

'You left the children alone downstairs. They could have wandered off anywhere, while you were away.'

'Tim was sound asleep, and I knew Holly wouldn't budge an inch until I brought her this,' Jay waved the toy bear in his face like a yellow banner. 'I only left them for five minutes. *You*,' another accusing wave, '*you* tried to refuse them a roof over their heads. And an unsafe roof it's proved to be,' she blamed him irrationally, feeling privately thankful that the roof in question had not turned out to be a thatched one.

'I want to talk to you about that.' Lyle put out his hand as if he might detain her, in spite of his criticism of her for coming upstairs in the first place, but Jay flung herself out of his reach as if she had been stung.

'I've said all I intend to on that subject,' she retorted defensively. Lyle had tricked her into remaining at Millpool Hall over night, and that one night was enough. More than enough, her throbbing pulse warned her. The few short, stormy hours under Lyle's roof had penetrated the barricades of her heart that had withstood years of willing suitors until now. 'I'm going,' she declared forthrightly. She had to go, before the barricades were collapsed completely by a man who had no desire to step over them. 'If you must talk,' her wary eye took note of the glint of anger in his, 'you can do so downstairs, after I've given Holly her toy.' She knew she would have no chance of flight if he insisted upon detaining her, and she dared not remain alone with him

while he talked. She needed the defence of other
people's company, the armour of distance between
them. She could not be certain of her own reaction if
Lyle should touch her again. Without conscious
thought her hand began to rise to cover her lips, that
still tingled with the memory of his kiss.

Slight though the movement was, he noticed it. Too
late, she checked her hand and saw by the quick gleam
in his eyes that he not only saw but accurately
interpreted the quick, upward lift of her fingers towards
her mouth, and his eyes mocked her for it, daring her to
complete the movement, and cover her vulnerable lips
with her equally vulnerable hand.

'He thinks I'm afraid he'll kiss me again.' Was she
afraid that he would, or was she afraid that he would
not? Her sharply indrawn breath hissed through her
teeth, and rich colour flooded her cheeks.

'J-a-a-y! I want my teddy!'

'Saved by the bear!' Jay thought shakily and took
advantage of the welcome interruption, as Lyle half
turned to catch the child's cry floating from downstairs.
'Coming, poppet!' With a quick movement she ducked
through the doorway under Lyle's outstretched arm,
and ran quickly away from him and down the stairs,
and despised herself for the wild palpitations of her
heart that forced her to lean across the door of the
kitchen when she reached it, and gasp for breath, before
she recovered sufficiently to cross the quarry floor and
tuck the teddy bear deep inside the blanket alongside its
small owner.

'Now go to sleep until breakfast time.' She dropped a
kiss on the fair, tousled head, and saw thankfully that
Holly's eyelids were already begining to droop.

'Have the firemen left the building safe?' She threw
the question at Lyle over her shoulder. She did not turn
round. She did not need to. Every nerve of her was
throbbingly aware of him behind her, watching her, his
eyes boring a hole in her back as she bent to lift the
drowsy child further on to the settle, and spoke as she
lifted, using words as a protection against him.

'Why doesn't he answer me ... say something?' she asked herself desperately. Her spine melted under the heat of his stare, and turned her trembling limbs to putty as it burned at her nerve endings until they were as useless as the snapped strings of a puppet doll, and incapable of responding to the urgent demands of her frightened mind to carry her from the room, quickly, before Lyle's silent stride could bring him across the quarry floor towards her, close enough to touch her. Tension cramped the muscles of her neck into an agonising knot when he still did not speak, and her fingers gripped the edge of Holly's blanket until her nails bit deep into the soft wool.

'Whatever's going on, Mr Lyle?'

Jay stared dazedly towards the outside doorway. A plump, white-haired figure blocked out the growing daylight. She blinked, and recognised the figure.

'There's nothing going on,' she thought raggedly. 'Nothing at all.' She opened her mouth to tell Martha there was nothing.

'I met the fire engine on my way in with the milk lorry, just now, and the smell of burning's fair awful in here.'

'She means the fire,' Jay realised hysterically. 'She means the fire, not Lyle and me.' Even as Martha's meaning penetrated her dazed mind, another thought followed on the first. 'What a blessing I didn't speak out loud!' Her cheeks burned at what Lyle would have thought, if Martha hadn't interrupted her indignant denial of 'goings on'.

'Lightning struck the old wing of the house during the storm last night,' Lyle explained the calamity, and walked across the room to join them.

'How much damage has it done?' Martha demanded practically, and hung up her coat on a hook behind the kitchen door and started to tie the strings of her apron.

'Extensive,' Lyle replied briefly. 'The roof's gone, and two of the ground floor rooms are badly damaged. The study's a mess, but the dining room's worse, it's almost gutted.'

It was as nothing to the damage that had been inflicted on her heart, but that did not seem to matter to anyone but herself, Jay thought bitterly.

'Eh, all that lovely old panelling!' Martha mourned.

'The panelling took the full brunt of the flames,' Lyle confirmed. 'In fact, it must have helped to spread them. It was hundreds of years old, and tinder dry, and the part of it that wasn't burned to a cinder is damaged beyond repair. What's left of the panels are hanging away from the walls like strips of old wallpaper. Until I've had time to assess the damage properly, I don't even know where to start to clear up the mess.'

'Start with a good breakfast inside you,' Martha answered him briskly, and produced a large saucepan from the nearby cupboard. 'Porridge, boiled eggs and batches, and some of that cherry preserve I made last autumn for your uncle. And after that, I'll go upstairs and get my old room ready,' she added in an offhand manner. 'I can help better if I live in than if I live out, and now the two children are here. . . .' She spooned oats into the saucepan with a 'that's settled, then,' manner that momentarily touched Lyle's lips with a quick, upward quirk.

'I'll bring your case back from the village for you as soon as you've had time to pack,' he offered gravely.

'I've never unpacked,' Martha returned gruffly, with her face to the range, and her back turned towards the room.

'Neither have I,' Jay cut in swiftly, 'so when you go to the village to collect Martha's case, you can give me a lift to the station at the same time. With Martha here to keep an eye on the children, there's simply no excuse to detain me a moment longer.' Unrepentantly she let Lyle know she saw it as an excuse, and not as a valid reason. 'Rouse up, Holly—Tim—you've got ten minutes to get washed and dressed before breakfast's ready!' The porridge would take longer than that to cook, the urgency was Jay's, to remove herself from the kitchen, and out of range of Lyle's inimical stare.

'It seems a shame for you to rush off so soon after

you've arrived,' Martha demurred. 'A day or two here would have rested you, after all that travelling.' Her tone made it sound as if Jay had covered the distance from the Gulf on foot, instead of in a jet airliner.

'My stay here's hardly been a restful one so far,' Jay directed her spleen at Lyle, and had the satisfaction of seeing his face tighten, but she went on unrepentantly, 'the children don't need me, they've settled down quite happily.' Why should she try to defend her desire to return to her own life? she asked herself angrily. Both Lyle and Martha seemed to be intent on making her feel guilty about wanting to leave, as if she was abandoning the two children, instead of merely leaving them with their rightful guardian.

'I've got my own work to complete.' She reminded them both sharply that there was another world beyond the boundaries of Millpool Hall and its estate. 'I have to take some scale drawings of stained glass windows back home to Chester, so that the workshop there can start on making the templates.' Her hard eyes told Lyle, 'I didn't lie when I said I was in the Gulf to sell stained glass windows to Arab sheiks.' Her look scorned him for his disbelief, as she herself would scorn to lie. 'There's no time to lose,' she went on quickly, before he could answer, 'the windows are due to be erected in the sheik's new residence by the end of the year.' There was plenty of time, the foundations of the residence were only just started when she left the Gulf, and the walls that were to support the windows were not even begun. She had already completed the drawings, even to the watercolour work, while she was still in the Gulf, so that her client would have some clear idea of what the stained glass windows in his new residence would look like when they were completed, and her earlier dedication to her task gave her ample room for manoeuvre now.

'Your side of the work's finished, now the scale drawings are complete,' her heart reminded her slyly. 'You could post them home just as easily, there's no necessity for you to take them yourself.'

'I need to discuss them with the others, to make sure they interpret what I've done in the way I want it,' Jay's mind defended her reasoning. It was not strictly true. She had not lied to Lyle, but she was lying to herself. Her architect father, and the craftsmen he employed, were more than capable of reading her immaculately executed sketches, and since she herself had been trained by her father, it was unlikely that John Baron would misinterpret any detail of her work.

'There'll be time for you to double-check when the full-sized cartoons have been completed by the workshop,' her heart persisted stubbornly. 'There's really no need for you to rush away from Millpool Hall, you could stay here and help Martha to clear up some of the mess caused by the fire.'

'I'm arguing with myself now, not with Lyle,' Jay realised desperately, and avoided the latter's eye when, much more than ten minutes later, she reluctantly returned to the kitchen with the two children, dressed, and ready for their breakfast.

'You'll need a good helping of porridge to warm you, those clothes won't do much to keep out the wind.' Martha placed steaming bowls in front of Holly and Tim and cast a critical eye on their lightweight garments.

'Beth didn't have time to buy them anything thicker,' Jay explained. 'They'd outgrown the clothes they took with them to the Gulf, and they weren't due to return to England for another two months, when the weather here would have been warmer. All their plans were set awry when the latest addition to the family decided to arrive early.'

Her own plans had been set awry, as well as Beth's, and if she did not leave Millpool Hall today, that very morning, her whole neatly ordered way of life was in danger of being badly disrupted for a long time to come. It would take that long, if ever, she felt unhappily certain, to get Lyle Gaunt out of her system.

'Until they're rigged out with some cosy woollies, they'd better play indoors,' Martha decided. 'I'll keep the range well stoked up, there's a big fireguard in the old nursery suite still, and a nice rug in one of the bedrooms upstairs, that's not being used,' she happily made plans to house her new charges.

'It sounds cosier already.'

Jay glanced up at Lyle, surprised by the unexpected warmth in his voice. 'He doesn't take after his Uncle Quintin,' she thought drily, and wondered if Lyle already had in mind a future mistress for his new home, someone who would supply the homely, feminine touches so clearly lacking now, and whose own children would one day play on the hearthrug.

'There's a queue forming outside already, to settle on the rug.' She checked the trend of her thoughts with hasty speech.

'The cats, you mean?' Martha's eyes twinkled at the feline line-up gazing in at them from the top of the garden wall. 'They're waiting for their morning helping of porridge, too. You can take it out to them, if you like,' she answered the eager looks of the two children, 'but mind and come straight back inside, out of the cold.' She handed the pair a tin platter each, and shooed them through the door.

'This one wanted to come in with me.' Holly returned first, clutching a half-grown black cat in her arms, that from its wild looks was not so enthusiastic about the arrangement as Holly would have them believe.

'The cats belong in the barns, not in the house,' Lyle frowned. 'Let it go, before it scratches you.'

'Surely the animal can't do any harm in the kitchen?' Jay protested. 'The place is almost as bare as a barn itself.'

'The cats aren't used to being picked up.' To Jay's surprise, Martha backed up Lyle's objection.

'She probably feels obliged to, now he's her employer,' Jay thought angrily. It seemed such a petty thing to do, to deny the child the cat to play with. 'Just because Lyle didn't want them to come, he needn't be spiteful now they are here,' she fumed, and ignored the patent truth of Martha's warning as the cat began to struggle in the child's arms.

'It knows it's missing its feed.' Martha began to look worried as the animal's writhings increased. 'It wants to go back to the others, before they finish all the porridge for themselves,' she coaxed Holly.

'I want it to play with.' The little girl hung on determinedly, and Jay's anger gave way to alarm as the cat started to growl ominously.

'Perhaps a plate of porridge to itself might tempt it to stay.' Swiftly she bent and placed her own half-finished bowl on the quarry floor, studiously avoiding Lyle's eye as she did so.

'Surely the child's got some rights in her uncle's house?' Hotly she defended her action as the cat slid free from Holly's arms, and cautiously approached the unexpected offering. 'If Martha won't uphold those rights, then I will, for the last few hours I'm likely to remain here,' she vowed determinedly. Just how many those hours were likely to be she had no clear idea, but Martha would need the contents of her case before the day was done, so Lyle would be obliged to go to the village to collect her luggage for her.

'He can take me to the train at the same time, whether he wants to or not,' Jay promised herself grimly. She did not look forward to the journey, short though it would be. The prospect of Lyle sitting tight-lipped and disapproving beside her made her wish she had sent her luggage on by carrier from the docks, which would have left her free now to assert her independence, and walk out on Lyle with her head in the air. But her suitcase was much too heavy for her to carry to the rail halt on the other side of the village, and it was too late now for her to regret her lack of foresight in not sending it on.

'If you've all finished, I'll get the washing up done, and then we can go upstairs to the old nursery suite, and find the fireguard, and maybe some toys in the big box there.' The motherly housekeeper tempted the attention of the children away from the cat in a way that set Jay's mind at rest about leaving them, and betrayed Martha's wholehearted welcome of the new regime.

It would not last for many weeks. Andrew and Beth would soon be back to claim their children, and then Martha would have Lyle on his own again. But by that time she herself would be back in Chester, immersed once more in her work, and the problems of Millpool Hall would be behind her. 'And forgotten,' Jay assured herself stoutly.

'Pass the plates along, Tim.' She joined in the clearing up, fighting the grey cloud of depression that descended upon her spirits at the knowledge that this was the first and the last time she would breakfast at Lyle's table.

'I'll take them.' Martha held out her hands for the stacked plates, and Jay lifted them carefully, and handed them over.

'Mind, they're heavy!'

'I've got them.' Martha turned towards the sink with her load. 'We'll soon be done with these, and . . . oh, drat the cat!'

Jay could not afterwards remember which came first, the cat's anguished squawl, Martha's equally anguished cry, or Tim's yelled, 'Be careful, you're stepping on the cat's tail!'

Crash!

The clatter of the breakfast crockery, meeting its fate on the unyielding quarry floor, effectively drowned all three, and the cause of it all, its black fur fluffed up like a bottle brush, fled through the door to the safety of its fellows in the yard.

'The cat finds the house as full of pitfalls as I do,' Jay sympathised, and for a brief, craven moment she longed to follow its precipitate flight. Lyle's face was thunderous. Jay glanced up and met his look, and quailed before the expression in his eyes.

'Are you all right, Martha?'

His voice was tight, clipped, and its tone cut short Tim's awed, 'Gosh! What a mess!'

'It's my ankle. I put my foot down awkward, like, to save myself from falling.'

'The cat shouldn't have been in the kitchen in the first place,' Lyle began, and Jay interposed hastily.

'Sit down, and let me have a look.' Years of independent travelling in the cause of stained glass windows had accustomed her to dealing with emergencies, and in the face of this one her mind brushed away the paralysis of Lyle's anger, and began to click over at its accustomed speed. With firm hands she guided the housekeeper to sit in the wheelback chair.

'Tim, get that broom and sweep up the broken crocks into the corner of the hearth. Don't try to pick them up, or they'll cut your fingers. Holly, kneel on the window seat and watch to see that the cat doesn't try to come back into the kitchen.' She gave both children a job to do, and added, 'Take your teddy with you so that he won't get brushed up as well,' ruthlessly using the child's attachment to her toy to force her to stay on the window seat out of the way. It was highly unlikely that the cat would want to come back into the kitchen, she thought balefully. Cats were sensible creatures, and the one just vanished would not risk an early return in the face of Lyle's wrath. His look boded ill for the one who caused the accident.

'Me!' Jay realised, with a cold feeling of dismay. The cat had not remained to reap the blame. It would be useless for Lyle to shout at Holly for bringing the animal indoors. Which left herself in the firing line. In spite of the glow from the range, Jay shivered as she knelt in front of Martha.

'Roll down your stocking and let me see.' Her voice did not betray her cowardice, she realised thankfully, as Martha dutifully rolled, and she ran seeking fingers over the abused ankle to assess the damage. 'It's beginning to swell.'

'I only ricked it,' Martha insisted. 'There's nothing broken, I'd know if there was. I just put my weight on the outside edge of my shoe when I felt the cat under me, and it turned my foot over.'

Her cheeks were a healthy pink, Jay saw with relief,

adding weight to her assertion that there was no serious damage done.

'Have you got a first aid box?' She gave Lyle a job to do as well, and felt a malicious satisfaction when he turned without speaking and obediently reached up to a cupboard fixed high on the kitchen wall.

'I'll put a firm bandage on it for you,' Jay decided, and wished her hands would remain as firm when Lyle kneeled down beside her and proceeded to open the lid of a brand new, comprehensive first aid kit that, she saw, had not previously been used. 'He brought it to the Hall with him,' she guessed correctly.

'Ordinary bandage, or crêpe?'

'Crêpe, I think.' Obviously he was prepared to postpone hostilities until Martha was made comfortable, Jay thought uneasily, and almost wished the storm would break over her head immediately, and be done with. Her hands fumbled with the paper wrapping on the bandage, trembling so that her fingers had difficulty in pulling it away.

'I wish he'd go away,' she thought crossly. 'Anywhere, rather than stay here watching me.' A surge of irritation took her, and she tore away the paper wrapping, and the small, soft cylinder of crêpe escaped, and rolled away across the floor.

'Bother!'

'Allow me.' He fielded it with a swift hand, and held it out to her, and a quick flush warmed her cheeks as she caught a glint of what could have been amusement deep in his honey-coloured eyes.

'He knows he's putting me off my stroke. He's enjoying it—doing it deliberately.' She reached out her hand and grabbed at the errant bandage, and her fingers met Lyle's as she took it from him.

'If I go on like this, I'll need first aid, as well as Martha.' The contact with his fingers was slight, but the effect upon her was electric. Jay felt as if she had been poleaxed. A violent tremor shook her, and she sat back on her heels, and somehow managed to retain her hold on the bandage, while the room swam in front of her eyes. She felt the colour drain from her cheeks, and hurriedly ducked her head over Martha's foot that rested on her lap.

'Hold the end of the bandage, Martha.' She could not see to hold it for herself. Her voice came out muffled, unsteady, and agonisingly her mind hammered a warning,

'I mustn't let Lyle see. . . .'

His eyes must not, and her own could not, she realised despairingly. Her shaking fingers ran along the injured ankle, feeling for the place to put the bandage, and the training of long-ago first-aid classes did the rest. She wound and smoothed automatically.

'Eh, but that feels a lot more comfortable.' Martha wriggled her encased member gratefully when Jay finished.

'It's more than I do,' Jay thought raggedly, and surveyed the neat figure-of-eight bandage with dull surprise. Her own hands must have wound it on. She did not recall them doing so. She only remembered the tension of Lyle's nearness, which still caught at her nerve strings, making them vibrate at his slightest movement like an over-tuned violin.

'You'll have to rest it for a few days.' Immediately she spoke, she saw the door of the trap she had laid for herself, and too late she tried to back away. 'I mean. . . .' She started to retract, but with swift inevitability Lyle pounced and slammed the door shut behind her before she could escape, and the look he slanted at her told her he would open it and release her only when he was ready to do so, and not before.

'Which means you'll have to remain here for exactly that length of time,' he told her decidedly. Told her, not asked her, she realised furiously as he snapped the lid of the first-aid box shut and rose to his feet to restore it to the wall cupboard. 'Martha can't possibly cope with two children until she's able to walk properly,' he added unarguably as Jay opened her mouth to protest.

'They could go to the village school.' She made a last, desperate attempt to escape.

'The headmistress won't take them this close to the Easter break.' He spoke over his shoulder, not even bothering to turn to look at her as he thrust his point home. 'She runs an educational establishment, not a crêche,' he reminded Jay forcibly, 'and even if she was willing to take them off Martha's hands, there's still the men to prepare meals for.'

'What men?' Jay snapped. She had only seen one man so far, and the more she saw of him, the less she liked him, her glare at Lyle declared.

'There's Mr Lyle, and the two farmhands,' Martha answered for him. 'And the herd.'

'Herd?' Jay echoed faintly. The farmhands she dismissed. They could bring their own food to work with them for a day or two. And as for Lyle, her lips compressed ominously, if he could not be bothered to prepare his own food, so far as she was concerned he could go without. But ... herd? 'I'm not mixing food for a herd of cows,' she declared forthrightly. Whatever other jobs Lyle might trap her into doing, playing chef to a herd of cows was not one, she vowed furiously.

'Herd—short for shepherd,' Lyle elucidated crisply, and Jay felt herself go limp. She felt an hysterical desire to giggle, and an equally pressing urge to cry. Willy-nilly, she was at Millpool Hall to stay until Martha was fully mobile again, and there was nothing she could do about it, and while her mind feared, her heart cheered the turn of events, and she despised them both, the one for its lack of courage, and the other for its treachery.

'What shall I do with the broken bits, Jay? I've swept them all into the corner, like you said.'

'I'll shovel them up and take them out to the dustbin,' Lyle answered the boy before Jay could speak.

'He might as well do the same with my feelings,' she told herself bitterly, and lest her thoughts should show on her face and betray her, she turned away, and called to Holly and Tim,

'Come with me and we'll go to find the fireguard.'

'Bob will come with you, and carry it downstairs for you,' Martha checked her impulsive move towards the stairs as a burly figure appeared at the kitchen door with his arms full of chopped logs.

''Mornin', gaffer—Martha.' He eyed Jay curiously as he dropped the logs into a big hod at the side of the hearth.

'Are your boots clean?' Martha questioned him suspiciously, and he grinned at her unabashed.

'I reckon so. The wind's dried out the yard. It's enough to cut you in two out there.'

'Then go along with Miss Jay and bring down the fireguard from the old nursery suite,' Martha bade him, and added, 'and the rug that's up there, as well, while you're at it.'

The housekeeper cut short the hand's goodhumoured grumble about the weather, and Jay quit the room along with him, thankful to turn her back on Lyle and the unbearable cross-currents of tension and antagonism that bade fair to do the same as Bob's wind, and cut her in two, she thought humourlessly.

'It's good to see children about the place. The Hall's been bare for too long.' Bob voiced his feelings cheerfully as Holly and Tim ran on ahead of them up the stairs.

'They won't be able to play outside until I've got them some warmer clothes,' Jay confided, grateful to relax in the farmhand's uncomplicated company. 'They'll have to be content to explore the toy box in the nursery until then.'

'Maybe you'll find a kite in there,' Bob suggested to an interested Tim. 'A March wind's a fine thing to make a kite fly.'

'If there's a kite, it'll be an old one, I expect, and probably broken,' Jay interposed doubtfully, unwilling to arouse the boy's expectations, and then see him disappointed.

'If you find a kite in there,' Bob shouldered the fireguard, and rolled the rug under his arm preparatory to departing kitchenwards, 'bring it to me and I'll fix it for you. And if there isn't a kite,' he forestalled the boy's eager question, 'come and let me know, and I'll make one for you,' and with a pleasant nod he left them.

'He's kind.' Lyle's harsh manner had left her unexpectedly vulnerable, and quick tears pricked behind Jay's lids. She blinked rapidly to clear them away. She must not let Tim and Holly see. They had sharp eyes, and were prone to make indiscreet comments, and she shrank from the humiliation of having her weakness paraded in front of their uncle.

'There *is* a kite, Jay. Look!' Tim drew out his find from the toy box triumphantly. 'Oh, the middle spar's broken. I wonder if I could bind it myself?'

'We'll take it downstairs, and ask Martha for some twine.'

'I've found a doll, and another teddy,' Holly piped up excitedly.

The toys were old, and much used, but they had the attraction of novelty, and the two children were soon playing happily with them on the rug in front of the newly guarded fire.

'What a difference a rug makes! The kitchen looks quite homely,' Jay exclaimed.

'Mr Quintin seemed as if he hated being in the house,' Martha excused her late employer's indifference to his lovely old home as she peeled potatoes with brisk efficiency into a bowl that rested on her lap. 'He had the rooms made comfortable for the cowman and his wife, and my own bedroom and small sitting room upstairs, but for himself,' she shook her head sadly, 'he used the kitchen, or his study, and then only when he had to. His whole life was spent out of doors, looking after his estate, particularly his pedigree herd. His home meant nothing to him.'

And all because the girl he loved had not loved him. Jay's heart twisted with sympathy that she refused to acknowledge might be akin to fellow feeling.

'I ought to be doing the vegetables for you,' she realised.

'I can do them well enough, sitting down,' Martha refused her briskly. 'Tim and Holly can fetch and carry for me. Though I'd be glad if you'd answer the telephone for me,' she cocked a listening ear as a shrill summons sounded from the inner hall. 'I never did get along with those things myself,' she grumbled. 'It doesn't seem natural, somehow, to talk to someone you can't see.'

'I'll take it,' Jay smiled, and returned a couple of minutes later with the message, 'It was the feed merchant from Millford, to say he'll be delivering Lyle's order this morning.'

'You'd better let him know right away,' Martha replied.

'Wouldn't it do when he comes in?' Jay objected. She did not want to go in search of Lyle. She did not want to face him again until she absolutely had to.

'Best not to risk it,' the housekeeper advised sagely. 'He'll want to make sure someone's around to take the sacks of feed when they come. If the merchant arrives and finds no one here to help him unload the lorry, he might go away again, and then goodness knows how long it'd be before he comes in this direction again.'

'And no doubt if he left without making his delivery, Lyle would blame me for that as well,' Jay deduced silently. The possibility of inviting further recrimination was even more unpleasant than facing Lyle in his present frame of mind.

'Do you know where he's likely to be?' she enquired reluctantly.

'He said he was going to have another look at the old wing, to see what can be done about starting to set things to rights again.'

'How . . .?'

'Instead of turning left for the stairs when you reach the hall, turn right and follow the long corridor.' Martha anticipated her question. 'The first two doors lead into the dining hall, and the third one into the study. Mr Lyle will be in one or t'other, I expect,' and she went on peeling the potatoes.

'Oh well, here goes,' Jay muttered. Following Martha's directions, she paused in front of the first door along the corridor. 'Lyle can't bite my head off for bringing him a message,' she scolded her own nervousness, and reached out a determined hand for the knob.

'Lyle?'

He turned slowly to face her, and the black devastation of the wrecked room was reflected in his eyes as he looked at her, and through her, hardly seeming to see her.

'Lyle. . . .' her breath caught in her throat, and she took a hesitant step across the scorched floorboards towards him.

'You should be with the children.' He spoke at last, curtly. His face was tight with weariness and strain, its expression closed against her. With an aching throat she longed to shout at him,

'Don't shut me out!'

But all she managed to utter was,

'The children are with Martha. I came to give you a message from the feed merchants in Millford.' In a strained voice, she gave him the messsage.

'I'll attend to it.' There was no change in his expression towards her, no expression in his voice.

'You might at least say thank you,' Jay snapped. She could not help it. Her fingers balled into tight fists at her side, that felt as if they battered in vain against the impenetrable barrier Lyle erected around himself, keeping her helplessly on the other side. Frustration stirred hot anger in her against his rocklike aloofness, that ignored the poignant pleading of her violet eyes, and told her plainly that he considered the burdens she would give her life to share were his, and his alone.

'Thank you.' His eyes returned from whatever inner vision they embraced, and fixed themselves with disconcerting directness upon Jay, looking at her, seeing her, mocking her futile anger against him.

'Thank you.'

Her own eyes faltered, unable to meet his stare. Desperately she wished she had not allowed her anger to get the better of her self-control, but it was too late now to wish. She had delivered the message from the feed merchant, and there was no longer any necessity for her to remain, but her feet seemed glued to the charred floorboards. As if in a dream she saw Lyle's hands begin to rise, and reach out towards her.

'He's going to kiss me again.' She watched them, mesmerised. 'I mustn't let him kiss me again. I can't bear it.' Her own unguarded tongue had invited his reaction, but it was too late to regret her impulsiveness. Perhaps—she cringed from the possibility—perhaps Lyle thought she had deliberately invited it, remembering his earlier taunt,

'No good deed should go unrewarded. . . .'

Her limbs felt paralysed as he gripped her and pulled her towards him, her face upraised in mute appeal because her voice refused to plead for her. With widening eyes she watched his head bend over her, blotting out the blackened room. His arms trapped her, holding her against him so that she was unable to move, and with slow deliberation his lips crushed down upon the trembling softness of her mouth with a fierce intensity that vibrated through her like a physical shock.

'The fireman was wrong. Lightning does strike twice in the same place.'

One last coherent thought pierced her mind with vivid clarity, before it succumbed to the onslaught of his kiss. Lightning struck the room she stood in, and now, in the same spot, it struck again, but its source was Lyle and not the elements, and all the water in the world could not quench the flame that rose within her, and threatened to consume her mind, her reason and her will. With terrifying speed it burned through her awakening senses, destroying her puny resistance, until with a small, inarticulate sound her resistance vanished, and she melted against him, drawn by the vital demand of his kiss as a moth is drawn to a flame, knowing the heat of it promised only pain and destruction, yet pulled inexorably towards the source of that destruction, and unable to help herself.

CHAPTER THREE

'THE window . . . the stained glass window!' Jay gasped. The coloured glass of the window swam into her line of vision like a lifeline, and she grasped at it desperately to save herself from drowning utterly in a whirlpool of emotion such as she had never experienced before, and into which Lyle's kiss hurled her without questioning if she could swim. The window looked as shattered as she felt herself. Half of its glass was gone. A detached part of her mind registered that, in what remained of the scene it once depicted, there was no lion rampant.

'Some of the glass could be saved,' she babbled.

Was it too late to save herself? The whirlpool spun her dizzily, and at such a speed as left no room for rational thought. Only for feeling, and her feelings were not rational, she tried to convince herself shakily. She could not possibly love Lyle. She had known him for less than twenty-four hours, and during that time they had quarrelled incessantly. She *must* not love Lyle. The consequences of loving him were too awful to contemplate, because he did not love her. His kiss meant nothing. A casual kiss meant nothing to a man, it was only a whim of the moment, that vanished as soon as the moment was passed. A violent trembling shook her like an ague, so fierce that Jay felt her teeth begin to chatter.

'Perhaps Lyle will put it down to the wind,' she thought hopefully, the keen fingers of the bitter March wind that whistled derisively through the gaping holes in the stained glass, where the heat of the fire last night had melted the lead, and loosed the lovely coloured segments to shatter on the floor below. Dazedly, Jay turned her face to meet the cutting blast, using the bitter cold of it as a restorative to clear her spinning head, and wished bleakly that she could find something

45

equally simple to restore her heart, that felt as shattered as the glass.

Her hands rose to cover her burning cheeks. For protection? Or for shelter? She dared not raise her eyes to look at Lyle. She could feel him looking down at her, his eyes piercing through her pressing fingers, but he did not attempt to touch her again. The moment had passed, for him. For herself? Jay closed her eyes, but her delicately veined lids were powerless to shut out the torment, so she opened them again and fixed them on the nearest recognisable object, and said in a voice she barely recognised as her own.

'Some of the glass could be saved.'

'It'll need an expert.'

She should have felt thankful that Lyle followed her lead. Instead, burning resentment fired her cheeks, that he could so easily dismiss what had just passed between them, shrugging off the moments of sweet intimacy as if they had never been.

'I *am* an expert.'

For the second time since she met him, she stated a bald truth in a voice—Jay felt at that moment as if she could pin a medal on her voice—that came out as matter-of-fact as the words it spoke. Gratefully she clutched at the firm, familiar ground of her work, letting it steady her shaking limbs, and enable her to turn at last and face Lyle, and make her claim with an outward calm that she hoped would deceive her listener, if it did not deceive herself.

'I'll need to engage an architect to put all this to rights.' He ignored her claim as if she had not spoken, and Jay bridled at his casual dismissal, but before she could let fly the angry words that tumbled to the edge of her tongue Lyle continued, 'I want someone who specialises in the restoration of old buildings. The whole house needs renovation, not just the damaged wing. The Hall's been neglected for too long.' His voice betrayed his infinite regret of such neglect, and the depths of his own affection for the ancient seat of his family. Through the armour of her anger, Jay felt a stab of envy for Millpool Hall. Lucky house, that it could so effortlessly win Lyle's affection! 'There are only a handful of men in the country who specialise in such work. The best of them, I understand, is . . . .'

'John Baron.'

They both spoke the name together, and Lyle paused, and directed a searching look at Jay.

'Of course, I'd forgotten, your own surname's Baron,' he said slowly. 'Are you, by any chance, related to the architect?'

'John Baron's my father.' It gave Jay immense satisfaction to claim the relationship. It punished Lyle for discounting her claim to expertise, and she lifted her chin proudly, conscious that she held his interest now. Bitterly conscious that it was not a personal interest, in herself.

'We,' she used the word deliberately, 'we employ a team of master craftsmen who specialise in this kind of restoration work. Stonemasons, wood carvers, and so on. I deal with the stained glass side of the business. No, not the actual physical work of putting it together,' as Lyle looked about to interrupt her, 'but the scale drawings, the coloured cartoons, and where necessary the research into the actual subject matter of the windows, since much of the work we do has a religious or historical inspiration, which covers a wide field, depending on which particular country the windows are destined for. Some, like your own, portray heraldic devices, or coats of arms,' she made a stab at what the design of the window might have been that the fire had so wantonly destroyed. 'It was just such an assignment that took me to the Gulf,' she reminded him with malicious pleasure, and her look challenged him to question her statement now, but instead he nodded, as if he had suddenly come to a decision, and said crisply.

'That simplifies matters. I'll engage your father's team to restore the Hall.' He spoke as if her father's acceptance of the work was a foregone conclusion, Jay realised indignantly, as if the possibility that John Baron might refuse the work did not even enter his mind.

'My father might not wish to accept the work,' she told Lyle with asperity. Her father was not just any architect, who could be engaged at the lift of a finger. He was in a position to take his choice from the stimulating assignments that regularly came his way, and it would do no harm, she decided sharply, to acquaint Lyle of the fact, that since John Baron's name had sprung so readily to his lips, he ought to have known already.

'Your father's fee will be quite safe.'

'How insufferably arrogant of you, to assume that the fee is of paramount importance when conjuring with a name like John Baron!' Jay flashed haughtily. Her eyes snapped as she continued. 'My father chooses his own assignments, without regard to the fee.'

'He won't have the opportunity to choose this one, unless he's told about it in the first place,' Lyle interrupted her curtly, 'so I suggest you telephone your father and let him know the work is available if he's willing to take it on. Or,' his voice hardened perceptibly, 'or shall I approach him myself?' when she made no immediate move to comply.

'I'll telephone him.'

She would have given all she possessed to tell Lyle to do his own telephoning, to refuse the job on behalf of her father, and walk out of the charred room with her head in the air, and her pride intact, but caution gave her pause. She had not the authority to accept or reject jobs on behalf of her father. That prerogative John Baron reserved exclusively for himself, and if subsequently Lyle did contact her father, and the latter decided to accept the assignment . . . Jay flinched from the humiliation of being overruled. Worse, her father might pass on instructions to herself, through Lyle. The possibility was not to be borne, so she said hastily, hating the capitulation, hating Lyle for being the cause of it.

'I'll telephone him.'

'If your father isn't able to accept the whole of the work, he might be prepared to take on the stained glass window alone. You could do the groundwork for that while you're here.'

Lyle was already giving her instructions! High-handedly assuming she would have no option but to carry them out. Jay's sturdy independence rose in rebellion, and she flashed back recklessly.

'I won't. . . .'

'You *said* you were an expert.'

His icy challenge stopped her in her tracks. It was as if he had flicked her across the face with the gauntlet, before throwing it down between them. She drew in a ragged breath, and fought for the composure to pick it up and fling back.

'I *am* an expert.' She tilted her chin proudly.

'Then prove it.'

'I'll prove it, if it's the last thing I do,' Jay breathed through gritted teeth. 'When I've finished with your window, it'll be better than it was before. I'll make you admit. . . .'

'That remains to be seen, when the work's completed.'

It was like pummelling rock. Her words made absolutely no impression upon their target. Lyle's face remained impassive, showing no reaction to her anger. He *was* rock! she fumed silently. Hard, and unfeeling.

'You'll have to use the telephone in the hall. The extension in the study is damaged beyond repair.' Relentlessly he drew her back to the task in hand, obliging her to comply with his wishes by the implied threat that, if she refused, he would contact John Baron himself. Tight-lipped, Jay swept past him and made her way to the telephone in the hall, willing her father to refuse the work with every number she dialled.

'Millpool Hall . . . you know, I wrote to tell you I was bringing Beth's children back with me.'

'Yes, I got your letter,' her father's voice confirmed. 'I looked up the place in the library. It's got a fascinating history.' Jay grimaced silently. Too well she knew her father's weakness for old country manor houses. 'It's mentioned in the Domesday Book.'

Doomsday would be a more appropriate spelling, Jay told herself bleakly, and said aloud,

'It'll be an insurance job.' Insurances usually meant long, frustrating delays before any work could be started. Perhaps the delay would deter her father, she thought hopefully. 'In any case, it's a comparatively small place,' she pursued doggedly.

'Not all that small.' Her father had done his homework well. 'And it's very old, according to the write-up.' Jay knew she had lost, even before he added, 'The house sounds a gem of its kind, and it could well repay our attention.' He did not mean in money, she knew. She had overlooked her father's sense of dedication to what he regarded as a national heritage. The house was indeed a gem. Not so its present owner, she decided caustically, and had one more try to sidetrack her parent.

'I've got to come back home first, with the cartoons I've done for that assignment on the Gulf.'

'You can post those on to me,' her father told her with misguided helpfulness. 'I'll take over when I receive them, and leave you free to stay on at Millpool Hall and do the initial survey work there. The insurance company is bound to want an estimate for repairs to the fire damage, and while they're making up their minds about that, you can carry on with surveying the rest of the house. Your task will be made that much simpler, since you're already friends with the owner.'

'With the owner's sister, but definitely not with the owner,' Jay muttered, and answered her father's, 'What did you say? I didn't quite catch. . . .' with a hasty, 'Oh, nothing. I was just thinking out loud, that's all.' Put baldly into words, particularly over the telephone, her battle of wills with Lyle would sound like nothing so much as an undignified sparring match. With herself, up to now, the loser, she acknowledged grimly.

'By the way, don't forget to consult closely with the owner at each stage of the survey.'

'I'll remember.' She shrank from the close encounter of long hours of detailed discussion with Lyle about the restoration of his lovely old home, whose future she would ensure, but not share. A home she would restore for another woman to eventually enjoy. Hurriedly she switched her mind back to what her father was saying.

'Remember the owner has the final choice of what work is to be done.'

'The owner has the final choice. . . .' Jay's heart contracted painfully. She would not—would never be—Lyle's choice. With an immense effort she forced herself to respond as John Baron outlined his suggestions for the work to be put in hand, and Jay gave an inaudible sigh of relief as they came to an end with the promise.

'I'll send the scaffolders out to you this afternoon. They'll put up overnight somewhere close enough to come in and start erection at first light tomorrow morning. You'll have a temporary cover erected over the damaged roof by midday tomorrow, and then the next step is up to you. Let me know if you meet any stumbling blocks.'

The only stumbling block was Lyle. He reappeared like an unwelcome shadow beside her as she put the receiver back upon its rest, and enquired in an expressionless voice.

'Well?'

'My father says he'll accept the assignment.' Stubbornly, Jay refused to associate herself with her sire's decision. 'He wants me to remain and do the initial survey.' Her look said she did not share John Baron's desire in that respect, either.

'Uncle Lyle, Martha says elevenses are ready, if you are.'

Jay regarded the boy's uncle over the rim of her coffee cup, and her eyes held the glint of battle.

'I can't possibly survey your house and look after two children at the same time,' she stated flatly. 'Let Lyle wriggle out of that if he can!' she told herself unrepentantly. He had deliberately pushed her into two jobs, and now he must retract on one of them. She could not—would not—attempt to do both.

'That's already attended to. . . .'

'I'm going to look after Tim and Holly, and glad to do it,' Martha put in happily.

'What about you ankle?' Jay protested.

'It's not so bad now it's got a bandage on. I can stand on it enough to look after the two children,' Martha smiled at the small pair, 'and I can do the cooking at the same time.'

'What about the housework?' Jay asked suspiciously. This was too much! she fumed. Whatever Lyle said, she did not intend to have the housework dropped onto her unwilling shoulders.

'I've arranged that, too.' Lyle neatly defused her mounting indignation. 'I've engaged a girl to come in from the village to do the rough, which will leave you free to do the survey work uninterrupted,' he finished evenly, and Jay bit her lip. He had got it all worked out. It was almost exactly what her father suggested. Everyone seemed bent on leaving her free to do the work they wanted of her, and took her own agreement for granted. Lyle had taken it very much for granted. He had not even waited for her to finish her conversation with her father, before deploying his household in a manner that would leave her free to. . . .

'Ssschwppp!'

'Tim!' Jay vented her ire on the young offender. 'Don't slurp your cocoa in that noisy manner. Drink it properly. What on earth would your mother say, if she could hear you make a noise like that?'

'Bob drinks his cocoa like that.' Tim's clear young voice defended his right to emulate the manners of his new hero, and Jay looked from one to the other, nonplussed. Since Bob offered to mend the boy's kite, he could do no wrong in Tim's eyes, but she blanched at the thought of what Beth would have to say if her son repeated his performance in her presence. But to scold Tim would be, by inference, to scold Bob as well, who still busily supped from his mug with the noisy enthusiasm of bathwater disappearing down a plughole, happily unaware of the consternation he was causing. Jay's face took on a hunted expression, and instinctively she glanced up at Lyle.

'He's laughing at me.' There was no mistaking the upwards tilt of his well cut lips, the gleam of amusement in his honey-coloured eyes that taunted her, 'Wriggle out of that, if you can!' Using her own tactics, to discomfit her. Jay's colour rose angrily, and she longed to slap all three, Tim and Bob both, but most of all Lyle, for putting her in such an impossible position.

'I can see the feed merchant's lorry coming through the yard gate.' Lyle cocked an eye out of the kitchen window, and directed Bob's attention to the vehicle nosing its way into the farmyard.

'I'll be off, then, gaffer. Thanks, Martha.' Bob put down his empty mug on the table, nodded cheerfully and left them, and Martha remarked into the speaking silence that followed his disappearing back.

'It's as well you decided to open the breakfast room, Mr Lyle, and have the meals served in there for yourself and Miss Jay and the children.'

Once more, Lyle had made arrangements on the assumption that her stay at the Hall would be long-term, Jay deduced sharply. And he had arranged it without any reference to herself. There was no reason why he should consult her in his own home, but illogically she resented the omission.

'You're a coward,' she lashed herself with silent scorn. She should have taken swift, decisive action, against Tim and Bob, and dealt with them both in a manner that would have told them, and Lyle, she was not to be trifled with. Instead she had remained ineffectually silent, until Lyle rescued her, and the laughter that lurked in the depths of his eyes mocked her for her inability to cope without him. Questioned her inability to cope alone, with her work on his home?

'I'll prove I don't need him,' she vowed, and felt a black cloud of depression descend upon her, because her triumph would also be her swan song, and the day she proved herself would be the day her work at the Hall was finished, and the time for her to leave it behind her forever, and face a future where she would

have to learn to cope without Lyle, but in which she
would never cease to need him.

'The insurance assessor is coming to look at the fire
damage this afternoon, Martha. I shan't be able to pick
up your case from the village until this evening.'

'It won't matter until tomorrow, Mr Lyle,' the
housekeeper assured him placidly. 'I left enough of my
clothes upstairs to see me through for a day or two.'

'In that case, tomorrow morning,' Lyle promised.

'Why not take Miss Jay with you?' Martha suggested.
'You could go on into town and get some warm
clothing for the children at the same time. I can't keep
them penned indoors indefinitely,' she pointed out
practically, 'and they can't play outside in thin cotton
clothes, in this wind.'

'We'll do that,' Lyle agreed, and a surge of angry
rebellion rose in Jay.

'No!' she exploded, in angry refusal, and became
conscious of two pairs of eyes pinpointing her. Martha's
held a look of mild surprise. Lyle's—she caught a quick
breath—Lyle's had a look of steely determination in
them. 'I'll be far too busy working on the survey,' she
defied the determination. She was here on contract on
behalf of her father's firm, not as a lackey to Lyle. 'Take
Martha with you instead,' she told him brusquely.

'Martha can't walk through town on a damaged
ankle.' The steel in Lyle's eyes hardened.

'Then take the children with you, and fit them out
there and then,' she retorted stubbornly.

'The children can't walk about town in cotton
clothes, in this temperature, any more than they can go
outside to play, for the same reason.'

Stalemate! It was not being fair to Tim and Holly to
deprive them, in order to give herself the satisfaction of
scoring off Lyle. Jay chewed her lower lip in angry
frustration. Once again Lyle was using moral blackmail
to force her to comply with his wishes, and she hated
him for pressurising her into a position where she could
not refuse. Into the fraught silence, she gave what she
hoped looked like an indifferent shrug, and said,

'It's the work on your property that'll be delayed, and my time you'll be paying for,' she reminded him maliciously, turning his victory into a minor one of her own, the while she wondered uneasily how far away 'town' was. She had no knowledge of the local geography, but however short the journey it would be much too long so far as she was concerned, with Lyle as her sole companion.

'What time are you expecting the insurance assessor, Mr Lyle?' Martha's eyes made a rapid survey of her luncheon preparations, patently wondering if she had sufficient to cater for another appetite.

'He said about two o'clock, when I rang him a few minutes ago.'

'That was quick, for an insurance company,' Jay could not resist commenting, and Lyle slanted her an oblique look.

'Naturally, he arranged to come as soon as possible, when he heard what had happened.'

'Oh, naturally.' The sarcasm in her voice was thinly veiled, and Lyle's eyes narrowed, but Jay ignored them and went on, uncaring, 'No doubt when a Gaunt requires assistance, the whole county jumps to attention.' Lyle was yet to discover that she did not number herself among them. If the insurance company assessor came doffing his cap, she, Jay Baron, was not prepared to do the same.

He did not wear a cap, and far from being elderly and obsequious as her imagination suggested, he was middle-aged and cheerfully efficient, and—a point that straightaway raised him in Jay's favour—he immediately recognised who John Baron was. Lyle said,

'I've contracted John Baron to do the work of restoration.' Not, Jay noticed indignantly, 'John Baron has agreed to accept. . . .' Her quick frown in Lyle's direction seethed with angry contradiction, but before she could give it voice the assessor said.

'Not *the* John Baron?' with an awed whistle that was balm to Jay's bruised pride, and the fury melted from her, and she smiled sweetly upon the newcomer.

'I'm Jay Baron.' She introduced herself, since Lyle did not seem to be in any hurry to do so. 'I'm here to do the initial survey work for our firm.'

'Not,' her barbed glance told Lyle, 'not to prepare your meals, or to run into town with you to purchase clothing for your niece and nephew, or to do any of the multitudinous tasks that you seem to take for granted I'll be willing to shoulder on your behalf.'

'Your being here will make my task much easier, as well as very pleasant, Miss Baron,' the older man assured her gallantly, and returned her smile with a look of open admiration on his face that brought a scowl to Lyle's as black as the storm that had wrecked his home.

'So Lyle's got a chink in his armour,' Jay saw gleefully, noting the scowl, brought about, she could only suppose, by having his own ascendancy over herself temporarily usurped.

'If you'll consent to accompany me while I inspect the fire damage,' the assessor invited her, unaware of the barbed undercurrents flowing around him, 'we can go over it together, and reach agreement at least on the salient points. That way, you'll make the final acceptance of your estimate by my company a matter of mere formality.' The expert from the insurance company did not doubt her capabilities, and Jay cast a triumphant glance at Lyle, but his face remained expressionless, refusing to register her triumph, and deflated, she turned and walked beside the older man towards the fire-stricken wing. Lyle did not second the assessor's invitation to accompany them, but Jay hardened her resolve, and went anyway, sheltering behind the other man's conversation, in which he included herself with flattering acceptance as a fellow professional, on site to assist a client, and she basked in the temporary sunshine of his approval, that was noticeably lacking in Lyle's treatment of her.

'What a mess!' The newcomer echoed Tim as he viewed the wrecked dining hall. 'That lovely old panelling, and the stained glass window,' he shook his head sadly.

'A lot of the glass can be saved, so be careful how you step,' Jay begged him. 'Some of the segments have fallen to the floor underneath the window panel, but not all of them are broken. I can rescue those, and the useable bits of the rest, to put back into the repaired window. Most of this,' she picked up a piece of blue glass and held it up to the light reverently, 'most of this must be the original glass, and practically priceless. We might be able to match some of it in our workshop, with bits we've salvaged from other jobs,' she finished hopefully.

'I can see your window is going to be as good as new, Mr Gaunt, when Miss Baron's finished with it.'

'Better than new,' Jay contradicted him firmly, and the assessor laughed.

'You can say that again!' he encouraged. 'In your hands. . . .'

'I've said it twice already,' Jay counted silently, and looked straight across at Lyle. Her words conveyed nothing to the other man, but she saw their meaning did not miss Lyle. His eyes locked with her own in a level stare, and the look in them repeated his previous challenge.

'Prove it.'

'You won't be able to salvage any of the panelling, I'm afraid, at least not on this side of the room.'

The assessor's brisk comment cut through the shackles of Lyle's stare, and Jay tore her eyes away, and forced them to look at the panelling, and felt as battered as the charred and twisted wood that hung away from the blackened walls as if seeking to escape the devastation of the flames, a ragged travesty of the once lovely polished oak.

'The minstrels' gallery is gone.' Lyle glanced upwards, and then down again as if he could not bear to look and Jay winced at the gaping hole that had been the gallery floor above them, support to long ago instrumentalists who nightly shed music on the diners below. For the first time, she realised the immensity of the dining hall.

'There was a screen to cut the room in half, for when the family dined alone.'

Lyle's words conjured up a scene of cosy intimacy, and Jay flinched away from the knowledge that her firm would have to replace the screen to afford Lyle's own family future privacy.

'As soon as this inspection's over, I'll have a plastic rick sheet tied across the roof to keep out the weather.'

'Plastic's no use,' Jay objected instantly. It was better to do battle with Lyle than to dwell on the unattainable, it did not leave so many scars. 'If there comes a high wind, plastic's likely to tear, it's more of a nuisance than it's worth, in the long run,' she insisted. 'I'm having a team of scaffolders sent down from Chester to erect a corrugated iron cover over the whole of the damaged area. The new roof can be built underneath the temporary cover, and it'll keep the place dry in the meantime.' Lyle should see she did not intend to be a mere cypher in the operation. He was the owner, but there, for the moment, his responsibility began and ended. She was in charge of the preliminary survey work, which meant providing any necessary protection such as covering against the weather, and since she was engaged professionally she intended to ensure the work was done in the way she wanted. Her straight look told Lyle plainly, 'I won't accept interference, even if you are the owner.'

'When will the scaffolders arrive?' The keen edge to Lyle's voice held a warning, but Jay was too busy defending her stand to notice.

'They're travelling down this afternoon, so that they can start erecting at first light tomorrow,' she answered him abruptly. 'We don't drag our heels, but equally we're not jet-propelled. My father only agreed to accept the contract a few hours ago.' Deliberately she rephrased Lyle's own interpretation of the agreement. 'Our men have to come from Chester,' she reminded him sharply.

'If it rains tonight, what's left of the contents of the rooms will get another soaking, and compound the damage,' Lyle pounced on her timing, and dismissed her explanation, and his tone bit as he added. 'It may have escaped your notice, but all of one side of the roof is open to the sky.' It had not escaped her notice. The wind, if nothing else, made the hole gapingly obvious, and Jay's lips tightened.

'The sky's clear enough,' she pointed out sharply. 'There hasn't been a cloud in sight since the storm cleared this morning.'

'The hills to the north of Millford make the local weather unpredictable.'

'Not only the local weather,' Jay muttered meaningly. Lyle was as likely to erupt as the elements.

'It's true, Miss Baron, the area's subject to sudden squalls,' the insurance assessor backed Lyle with his local knowledge.

'I've encountered several already,' Jay retorted meaningly, and sensed the first rumblings of yet another when Lyle replied with a flat statement that brooked no argument.

'Which is why I intend to have a rick sheet tied in place the moment this inspection's over.'

To Jay's tensed nerves, the inspection seemed to go on for hours. In reality it could only have lasted little more than three. The assessor finished with the dining hall, agreed on the main points that would have to be dealt with, decided which furniture could be salvaged, and which was beyond hope. Jay mourned with him for the beauty of the antique carved oak, that had stood the siege of centuries, and succumbed in a single night to the flames. She winced away from the analogy with her own heart, and followed the men with dragging feet into the study.

'The damage here's not nearly so bad.'

But quite bad enough, Jay saw. In common with the dining hall, the roof had suffered the worst, and the leaded lights in the window were gone, but there was no stained glass panel in this one, and the contents of the room had suffered more from the intense heat and smoke, then from the flames themselves.

'Everything looks scorched to a crisp, but with time and skill the furniture could be made as good as new, wouldn't you say, Miss Baron?'

'Most of it seems to be surface scorching only,' Jay agreed, running her fingers experimentally across the carved back of a chair. Fingers that trembled with the knowledge that the lightning that had struck herself had burned far deeper than the surface, and the scars it left would not be so easy to eradicate.

'The bookcase and the desk seem to be the worst hit, being nearest to the outside wall,' the assessor observed. 'Was there anything of particular value in them, Mr Gaunt?'

'The leather-bound volumes held the estate records, and more important, the detail history of the pedigree herd,' Lyle answered, indicating a row of volumes lining the top two shelves of the bookcase. Faintly through the stains of soot and water Jay could detect dates on the spines of one or two of those least affected.

'One book for each year,' she deciphered, through screwed-up eyes.

'My uncle kept a detailed record from the first bottle reared calf with which he started the herd fifty years ago. The information it contained was invaluable, and since there isn't another copy, it's irreplaceable as well. For the sake of a few minutes in time, a lifetime's work has been destroyed,' Lyle finished bitterly.

'And he blames me, as being the cause of the destruction.' Like an accusing finger his words came back to haunt Jay.

'The fire wouldn't have gained such a hold, if I hadn't had to waste time rescuing you and the children!'

Would the records have been saved if the fire had been brought under control earlier? Would that vital ten minutes have made so very much difference? Lyle's set face said it would, and anger flared in Jay at the injustice of his accusation.

'Damaged, but not destroyed,' she insisted, refusing to accept his blame. Blaming Lyle for a wrong sense of priorities. 'The children are more valuable than a lot of

dusty old records,' she stated clearly, to the evident
bewilderment of the assessor, but not, she knew
caustically, to Lyle. 'If they'd been caught in the heat
and the smoke, they wouldn't have come through in
such good condition as the volumes,' she reminded
him grimly.

'Do you call this being in good condition?' Lyle
thrust one of the worst afflicted copies towards her, and
clapped it open with the palm of his hand. Water ran
forlornly down the inside of the cover, and dripped
through his fingers. Black, sooty water, that seeped on
to the brown, scorched pages, crinkling the edges until
they broke off in tiny wet flakes, that clung to Lyle's
skin as if reluctant to part from the rest of the page.
'The writing's practically indecipherable,' he growled.

'But not quite.' In a shaft of light striking down from
the glassless windows, Jay's keen eyesight caught the
faint outline of a once bold script. 'Don't shut the book
again,' she begged Lyle urgently. 'Leave it open, and let
it dry. Give it to me.' Desperately afraid that her plea
would cause him to do just the opposite of what she
asked, she grasped at the edges of the hide cover nearest
to her. 'Treat it gently,' she begged.

'What's the point?' Lyle refused to let go of the book,
and disconcertingly Jay found herself face to face with
him across the scorched pages. 'You can see the thing's
a write-off.' His tone said, 'Don't try to back out of
your responsibility for the damage,' and Jay controlled
her temper with an effort.

'I can make out the faint outline of some writing,' she
insisted. She could have shaken him for his refusal to
listen. 'Here . . . and here.' Stubbornly she still clung
with her one hand to the book, making sure that Lyle
could not slam it shut again, while with her other she
gentled the scorched page up to the light, letting it shine
through the embattled paper and highlight the bolder
strokes of writing that were still faintly discernible.

'Faint outline's an understatement!' Lyle gave a
harsh bark of a laugh that held no humour in it. 'The
writing's barely visible, and there are two shelves full of

books in this condition, and worse. It's an impossible task,' he declared impatiently.

'With the human eye, yes,' Jay acknowledged, 'but with micro-film it can be done.' She met Lyle's incredulous stare with the confidence born of knowledge. 'There's a special micro-film process that can pick out lettering which is practically invisible to the human eye. We're in touch with a specialist in Chester who's done similar work for us in the past, with excellent results,' she emphasised, determined to break through the barrier of Lyle's blame, to make him see that she was not just telling him this in order to justify herself.

'It's amazing what modern science can do,' the assessor murmured admiringly.

'It's a long process,' Jay replied, but she did not look at the speaker, her eyes held Lyle's, trying to bore through the barrier to reach him. 'Each separate page has to be thoroughly dried out before it can be micro-filmed, and then finally reproduced. It wouldn't be so satisfactory as having the original,' she acknowledged, 'but at least you'd have a readable photographic copy of the estate records.'

'Go on.'

At least he was listening. She went on, her words stumbling over themselves to prevent Lyle from slamming the covers of the book shut, and causing further, perhaps irreparable damage to the contents. 'The scorching has made the pages fragile, they'll have to be handled with the utmost care or they'll disintegrate. See, they've already started to crumble at the edges, where the water's reached them.' His eyes flicked down, noting the crumbling, and returned again to her own, and Jay caught her breath, and knew what a butterfly must feel like, pinned to a sample board, without hope of escape. 'It'll be an expensive process,' she babbled on, committed to the path that must prove her worth to Lyle, and at the same time exonerate her from the blame for the extent of the fire damage.

'The insurance cover should take care of any expense incurred.'

She hardly heard the assessor's reassurance, as she stared defensively up at Lyle.

'If these records are as valuable to you as you say they are——' her expression said clearly she did not believe they were. It accused him of using the damaged volumes as an excuse, a weapon with which to punish her for something that was not her fault. 'If these records are as valuable to you as you say they are, then release the books to me, and I'll send them back to Chester and have copies made that will be as good as, if not bêtter than, the original,' she challenged him fiercely.

CHAPTER FOUR

'IT's been a pleasure to meet you, Miss Baron.'

Jay felt her hand enfolded in the assessor's warm clasp, and wished wistfully that Lyle would say the same.

'I'll let you know the moment I've finished my estimate,' she promised, and willed the older man to remain for just a little while longer. Her mind panicked away from the prospect of being left alone again with Lyle.

'I think we've covered all the main points between us,' the former said heartily.

'I don't know. . . .' Jay frowned, and tried desperately to think of one more point that they could reasonably discuss between them. Nothing came. Her mind was a complete blank, aware only of Lyle standing tall, and silent, beside her.

'Thank you for coming.' He broke his unnerving silence, and held out his hand to the assessor.

'One day I'll make him thank me for coming,' Jay promised herself fiercely, and then remembered with a pang that the day her wish was fulfilled would be the day she departed from Millpool Hall. She tried to thrust the thought out of her mind with the same desperation that she had tried to will other thoughts in, and with as little success. Through a deepening cloud of depression she heard the assessor say,

'I'll be away now. From the size of the vehicle coming up your drive, Mr Gaunt, I reckon he'll want my parking space, and a bit more besides.'

'It's the scaffolders.' Jay could have laughed out loud with relief as she recognised the large covered van feeling its way round the bend in the farm drive.

'They've come too late to start erecting tonight,' Lyle observed. 'It'll be dark in an hour.'

'They won't try to erect tonight,' Jay retorted promptly, stung by his implied criticism. 'They'll unload tonight, and start erecting first thing tomorrow morning. That is, unless you want them to work by floodlight. The decision's yours, since you'll have to pay the extra.' Sharply she thrust the onus back on to Lyle.

'That won't be necessary.' He gave her a long, even look, and added deliberately, 'The plastic rick sheet will serve as an adequate cover for tonight.'

''Evenin', Miss Jay.'

'Hello!' Jay spun away from Llyle and ran towards the approaching van, her welcome over effusive to cover the angry colour that flooded her cheeks at Lyle's deliberate taunt about the rick sheet. Was ever a familiar face more welcome? she asked herself, and felt a curious lump in her throat as the bald head of the driver leaned out from his cab and asked her cheerfully, 'Whereabouts can we drop our load?'

'Over by that wall will do, for tonight.' She spoke quickly, conscious of footsteps behind her, determined that Lyle should not usurp her authority and give the driver instructions himself, rawly conscious of Lyle moving close against her shoulder, of the dominant male presence of him that would make itself felt even if she had her eyes shut, she thought uneasily, stirred by the now familiar mixture of confusion and resentment and something else that she did not want to recognise, that his close proximity aroused in her.

'If you drop your load against the wall, it'll be right in the path of the herd when they come in for milking,' Lyle warned easily, and Jay's cheeks lost their bright colour and turned white.

'Where, then, guv'nor?' To her chagrin the driver turned naturally to Lyle for directions. She opened her mouth to forestall his answer, but Lyle spoke first.

'Round the other side of the building would be best.'

'Was it necessary for you to countermand my instruction to the driver?' Jay turned on Lyle furiously as the van rolled away. 'Surely the equipment wouldn't have been in the way under the wall for just one night?

I'm in charge of the survey,' she reminded him hotly, 'and the men can't possibly work under two lines of authority. Particularly conflicting authority,' she condemned his intervention as high-handed interference in her domain.

'Unless you move to one side pretty smartly, the men will soon have only one line of authority left,' Lyle grinned, and put his hands round Jay's waist and pulled her without warning back against him.

'Don't. . . .' Anger did not armour her against his touch. The grip of his fingers felt like a ring of fire round her waist, and she tried to jerk herself away from him with a convulsive movement like a snared wild creature, terror-stricken by the force which held it, and helpless to break away.

'Stand still, or you'll get trampled,' he commanded, and held her with an easy strength that made light of her struggles to be free.

'Goo-ern. . . .'

Without warning a mass of black and white bodies lumbered round the corner of the wall towards them, urged on by the voice of an unseen man from somewhere behind, a solid, magpie-coloured phalanx of lowing heads and pattering hooves that advanced in an unbroken, jostling line. Jay's eyes grew wide with alarm, and she was unable to restrain a strangled gasp.

'Stop them!' She tugged at Lyle's arm in her urgency. 'Shoo them away. Do *something*!' she begged him shrilly, and when the leading cow began to trot, encouraged by the voice from behind the herd, her courage broke, and with a muffled sound she turned and hid her face in Lyle's jacket, her pride and her anger submerged in a wave of terror as the cows came towards them with a rush, eager for the shelter of their sheds, and their evening feed.

'Sit on the wall, you'll be safe there.' Incredibly a laugh rumbled through Lyle's chest, and she felt his arms lift her, and the round stone coping of the wall that divided the farmyard from the kitchen garden struck cold through the seat of her slacks.

'Don't let go of me!' She clung to him, cravenly, afraid he might leave her perched on the wall, and go away to deal with the rick sheet. Afraid that she might fall into the stream of Friesians still flowing below her. Would they never come to an end?

'Keep going, Daisy, you're holding up the line.' Calmly Lyle slapped the leader's black and white flank. 'Take them away, Shep,' he guided the collie that had the same colouring as the herd, and with an ease that if she had been farther away Jay would have found a joy to watch, the dog turned the leaders across the yard, and blessedly away from the wall, towards the sheds on the other side.

''Evenin', gaffer—Miss Baron.' The urging voice became a man with large wellington boots and a friendly smile, then unbelievably the heard was past them, and Lyle reached up and lifted Jay down from her perch on the wall, and said gravely, looking searchingly into her white face, 'Cows are no respecters of persons—or scaffolding poles,' and she looked back at him dumbly, and could not find an answer because she was trembling all over, and her throat felt parched, and she did not know whether it was from fright, or because Lyle held her, and she dared not try to find an answer to that.

'Where would you like the salvage boxes put, Miss Jay?'

The van driver rescued her. He rounded the wall, calling for instruction, and hastily Jay pulled herself away from Lyle, and hoped the man had not witnessed her shame, or Lyle's arms round her, or. . . .

'In the smaller of the two damaged rooms. In the study,' she called back to him breathlessly, forcing the words out quickly before Lyle could speak, before it became a recognised thing that the men would accept their instructions from him, and not from herself.

'Salvage boxes?' Lyle raised questioning eyebrows, and Jay felt a small satisfaction that this time it was he who was at a loss. It helped somewhat to even the score between them.

'They're boxes with soft padding inside them, for packing damaged goods that have to be sent back to our workshops for repair.' Here at least she was on familiar ground, and she talked on, relishing the firmness of it after the emotional quagmire in which she had floundered from the first moment she set eyes on Lyle. 'It's routine procedure for the first person on site to bring the boxes along in case they're needed,' she explained. 'In this case,' she added meaningly, 'if you want your estate records micro-filmed, the boxes will be put into use immediately.' Her words, her look, challenged him to admit that old estate records, even records of a pedigree herd of cattle, did not warrant such specialised attention, that they were not so important to Lyle as he would have her believe.

'I want them micro-filmed.'

His words were a flat statement. An admission? Or an instruction? Jay looked up at him sceptically, but his face gave nothing away, and after a long second of hesitation she shrugged, as if it was a matter of indifference to her either way, and said,

'In that case, I'll start to pack the volumes right away. They can go back to the workshops when the scaffolders return tomorrow.' Action would occupy her hands, and with luck control their trembling. She tried to feel elated that Lyle had accepted her recommendation about the estate records, but felt only a bleak emptiness descend upon her as Bob appeared from out of one of the farm buildings on the other side of the yard, and started to walk towards them, and Lyle hailed him with,

'Bring a rick sheet along with you, and come and help me to cover the damaged roof. I'll go and set up a couple of ladders.' He spun on his heel and left her, and Jay turned away with the driver to show him the way to the study, conscious of an intense aloneness because Lyle was not beside her.

'It's a good thing you were here when it happened, Miss Jay,' the man viewed the damaged study with experienced eyes. 'It isn't often a member of the firm's actually on site to pick up a job, so to speak.'

A good thing from whose point of view? Jay wondered cynically. Certainly not from her own.

'Do you want any help with packing these books, miss?'

'No, you go and help your mate to unload the van, then call it a day.' More than anything else, she wanted to be on her own, to recover her poise before she had to face Lyle again. 'You'll have an early start tomorrow,' she softened her refusal to make it look like consideration for the men, and thrust down a pang of conscience at her own deception.

'We've got rooms at the pub in the village, so we're practically on the doorstep. But if you're sure?'

'Positive, thanks.' The driver whistled away, and Jay took a deep breath and reached out towards the bookcase for the nearest of the volumes. It dripped sooty water on to her hand as she lifted it up, and she opened it and pulled a handful of wadding from the nearest salvage box, then dabbed up the surplus moisture, drying it as best she could without risk to the brittle, scorched pages inside. When she had finished she laid it in the salvage box, padding it carefully top and bottom, and reached out for another, working steadily along the shelves until their contents gradually grew less, and the salvage box beside her began to fill.

'This is the only way I'll survive the next few weeks,' she muttered through gritted teeth as she worked. The only way open to her, to fling herself into her work and use the intense concentration she knew would be necessary, in order to push all thoughts of Lyle from her mind. How else would she be able to endure the endless days that stretched ahead, when of necessity she must be in constant contact with Lyle, obliged to appear cool, and professionally detached, and all the time agonisingly conscious that one look from him, the accidental brush of his fingers against her hand, had the power to reduce her limbs to jelly, and her heart to palpitating malfunction.

'Ooh, it's cold!'

She sat back on her heels and blew on to her frozen

fingers, wishing her recent assignment had been in the Arctic Circle instead of the Gulf. The contrast in temperature was too great, although her stay in the sunshine had been of much shorter duration than that of the two children, and she had found the clothes she wore at the moment quite adequate before her departure from England. They did nothing to protect her now from the icy wind that whistled through the glassless windows, and remorselessly searched out every corner of the damp and freezing room.

'Leave the rest of the books until tomorrow!' Without warning a voice boomed from above her, seeming to come from outer space, and Jay started violently, and stared wildly round her. 'I'm up here,' it said, and she looked above her head and saw Lyle's face peering down at her through the hole in the roof. The effect was uncanny. It was as if he hovered above her, his head and shoulders blocking out the sky, and her eyes fixed wide and startled on to his.

'How long have you been up there?' Fright sharpened her voice. She had not heard him before he spoke, he could have been there for seconds or for minutes, she had no idea which. She spoke again with a quick frown. 'Why didn't you call out and let me know you were up there?' she asked him sharply. It was an intrusion to watch another person without their knowledge. It amounted to spying, and she resented being spied upon, particularly by Lyle. 'I don't like being spied on while I'm at work,' she told him shortly.

'If I'd called out to you, I might have made you jump and drop one of the books,' he justified his silence. 'You told me they'd have to be handled with the utmost care, or they'd disintegrate,' he reminded her slyly, and Jay's lips thinned.

'Just the same. . . .' The small fright had made her edgy, and she did not feel in a mood to forgive Lyle for being the cause of it.

'Loose out a bit more of the rick sheet to me, gaffer. It don't quite cover this side of the roof.' Bob's voice cut across her protest, and Lyle stopped looking down at her and straightened up, his face disappearing from the hole. Jay could see the top of the ladder that supported him above her, and her nervousness erupted in a bubble of relieved laughter that fought its way to the surface, and threatened to break through her stiff lips. Swiftly she pressed her frozen fingers hard against her mouth, and pretended to blow on them again, so that if Lyle glanced down at her he should not suspect their real purpose was to subdue the laughter at all costs, because it held more than a hint of hysteria in it.

'There'll be plenty of time to finish the rest of the books tomorrow morning.' Lyle's face reappeared at the hole, and Jay wished fervently that Bob would be quick and fix the rick sheet across it, and cut her off from Lyle's view. She felt like an insect under a microscope under his steady stare, and she wriggled irritably, to rid herself of the feeling, and retorted stubbornly.

There aren't many of the volumes left to finish.' Deliberately defying him, she reached out her hand to take another one from off the shelf, and felt herself begin to tremble again the tremor made her hand clumsy, and she fumbled at the hide cover of the book, that was made slippery by the water from the firemen's hoses.

'It'll soon be too dark for you to see properly what you're doing,' Lyle insisted, and Jay's ragged nerves gave way.

'I'd be able to see a lot better if you weren't blocking out the light from above me,' she cried in exasperation, and grabbed at the volume as it slipped from her nerveless fingers. Her clutching hands missed the spine, and slipped off the outer covers, which parted and let her hand down hard on top of the scorched pages inside.

'Now look what you've made me do,' she shouted at Lyle in exasperation. The top page, toasted to a crisp by the heat, cracked in all directions under the sudden blow, and she surveyed it with wide-eyed dismay.

'I told you to leave the rest of the books until

tomorrow,' Lyle began critically, and Jay flung back her head and flared up at him furiously.

'It wouldn't have happened if you hadn't been hovering over the top of me, shouting instructions,' she cried angrily. 'Go away, and do your own job, and leave me in peace to do mine!' Suddenly her voice trembled, perilously close to tears. It was diabolical luck that she should be the one to damage the book, when she had been at such pains to insist to Lyle that the volumes must be handled with infinite care. It was an even worse misfortune that he should be there to witness her clumsiness. 'Go away!' she choked, and ducked her head over the cracked page, and blinked rapidly to clear her blurred vision, while her shaking fingers sought to ease the broken sections of the page together again so that she might close the covers on it without doing yet more damage to the brittle contents.

'Take over on this side for me, will you, Bob?'

'Aye, gaffer. Leave the ropes dangling, I've tied the sheet down on my side now.'

Jay hardly heard the exchange going on above her. She felt rather than saw Lyle's face disappear from over the hole, and the rapidly departing daylight dimmed still further as Bob slid thick agricultural plastic to cover the gap, making her feel curiously cut off, when she should have felt only relief at the privacy it afforded her.

Impatiently Jay brushed the back of her hand across her eyes, refusing to dwell upon the feeling, and concentrated her cleared vision on the damaged page. It was not so bad as she had feared. The scorched page was cracked into three, but the separate pieces had not crumbled, and hardly daring to breathe, she gentled the edges together again and closed the covers of the volume over them with infinite care, and laid it carefully alongside its fellows in the salvage box.

'Let that be the last one for tonight.'

'Oh!' Jay gave a startled gasp. She had not heard Lyle approach, his soft-soled shoes crossing the study floor gave her no inkling of his presence until he stood over her, his hand reaching down to draw her to her feet.

'You've done enough for one day.' Masterfully he pulled her upright, heedless of her protest, and with his one hand he held her against him while he reached down with the other and closed the lid of the salvage box with a decisive snap, and observed critically, 'You're frozen to the bone.'

'That can't be helped.' Jay fought back with words. She did not feel frozen any longer. Lyle's touch set her on fire, the glow of it sent her pulses leaping with a wild abandon that drove the blood into her extremities, and set her fingers tingling. Irrationally they tingled with the urge to run through the crisp auburn waves of his hair, to trace the lean, clean outline of his jaw. She thrust her hands behind her back, and twisted her fingers together to subdue the urge, arguing stubbornly, 'I've got to get the books packed so that the scaffolders can take the boxes back with them to Chester when they've finished erecting tomorrow.'

'There'll be time in the morning.'

'You wanted me to go into town with you in the morning, to get clothes for the two children,' she reminded him with asperity. 'You can't have it both ways.'

'I shan't be free to go out myself until after the milking's finished. You can do the books while I'm busy in the dairy,' he deployed her time with an easy assurance that lit a spark of rebellion in Jay.

'There might be more than just books to go back to Chester.' Feverishly she wished she could pack herself safely in a salvage box, and go back to Chester as well, and perhaps salvage her pride, if not her feelings. 'There's the rest of the study to go through yet.' She flung a comprehensive hand at the old-fashioned rolltop desk, a long chest that acted as a window seat, and another bookcase that took up most of the wall on the opposite side of the room, all damaged by fire and water, and all mutely demanding her attention.

'The work can't all be done at once.' Lyle spoke as if

he was trying to reason with a wilful child, and Jay
bridled angrily. 'You'll have to be content to send on
the books first, and anything else must follow later,' he
said, and added firmly as she was about to speak, 'I'll
go through the rest of the contents of the study with
you, bit by bit, when I've got the time.'

'The work can't be put off until you've got the time,'
Jay butted in forcefully, stung by his casual assumption
that she would have to await his convenience to
complete the rest of her survey. 'I'm not prepared to
remain here indefinitely,' she declared independently.
'We do have other assignments besides Millpool Hall.'
She wanted to remain for ever, but since that was
impossible, the quicker she was able to complete her
work and leave the less it would eventually hurt. 'The
insurance company will expect my estimate within a
reasonable time,' she pointed out the obvious, using
words as a shield to cover the hurt that already lay deep
beneath the surface, and that no amount of distance
between them could heal.

'We'll make sure the insurance company isn't kept
waiting,' Lyle assured her gravely. Was he agreeing with
her? Or mocking her? Jay could not be sure. The
growing dusk shadowed his face, making it difficult to
read his expression.

'After that, there's the survey to finish on the rest of
the house.' She talked on desperately, defending herself
with words from the silence that must not be allowed to
drop between them, because silence between herself and
Lyle became filled with words she dared not speak, and
hopes which must remain unuttered, and she must not
betray her hopes to Lyle.

'There'll have to be a contract, drawn up and signed
to cover the work on the Hall.'

The contract her heart desired would need only the
simple, spoken words, 'I will. . . .'

'If it eases your mind, I'll send a letter of intent to
your father to carry through until a contract can be
signed between us.' The intent in Lyle's eyes was clear
enough as he bent his head above her, and said softly,

'In the meantime, a verbal agreement between us will have to suffice.'

'You mean a—a—gentleman's agreement?' It was a silly thing to say. She tried to strain away from him, her heart doing even sillier things inside her breast, that rose and fell unevenly in time to her panting breath.

'I wouldn't put it quite like that.' Quick laughter flared in his honey-coloured eyes. 'Gentlemen seal their agreements with a handshake. I'd hardly call that appropriate between you and me, would you?'

He gave her no time to answer. His hands firm against her back gave her no chance to get away. Unhurriedly he drew her close against him, and with slow deliberation let his lips act as a substitute for a handshake.

'Does that seal our agreement to your satisfaction?' he asked her at last, and before Jay could collect her wits sufficiently to tell him yes or no, he occupied her mouth again, exploring its soft fullness with a thoroughness that denied her the ability to answer, even if she had been capable of doing so.

As if in a dream Jay felt his arms slide right round her, enclosing her, while the pressure of his lips changed and deepened, searching her own hungrily until, with a soft moan of submission, she ceased to strain away from him, and felt herself go limp in his arms, arching her head backwards the better to reach up and taste the forbidden sweetness of his kiss. Somewhere in the remote background of her consciousness she knew that what she did was madness, that in weakly allowing herself to respond to Lyle's caress she sealed, not an argument between them, but her own fate, because now, no matter how soon she left Millpool Hall behind her, nor how far away she journeyed, she knew with a despairing sense of inevitability that Lyle's shadow would always travel beside her—the shadow of what might have been.

The plastic rick sheet flapped with monotonous persistence in the keening wind, and a patter like that of thousands of tiny feet vindicated Lyle's insistence on

covering the roof before it got dark. Rain. It sounded as
if it was pouring down. Jay turned over restlessly, and
pulled the bed covers over her head to try to shut out
the sound, and tried with as little success to shut from
her mind the unpleasant picture of what further damage
a soaking night might have caused the contents of the
otherwise exposed rooms if her own will had prevailed,
and the emergency covering had been left until the
following day.

Every now and then a dull thump punctuated the
other sounds, as if one of the ropes attached to the rick
sheet had come loose. 'I'll tell Bob about it tomorrow,'
Jay promised herself, and plumped her pillows for the
umpteenth time in a desperate attempt to woo sleep.

'Jay?' Tim must have heard her bed creak under her
restless tossing, and his cautious whisper quested
through the open communicating door between the two
rooms.

'What is it?' Jay slid out of bed instantly, and reached
for her wrap. 'What are you doing out of bed?'

'I want a drink of water, but I can't find the light
switch, and I've bumped my toe against something.'
The whisper became aggrieved, and the young sufferer
hopped on one foot to prove his injury.

'Never mind, snuggle back under the blankets, and
I'll bring you a drink across.' Jay scoooped him up and
slid him back into bed, and filled a beaker from the
pitcher on the marble topped wash stand.

'I'll sit with you while you drink it.' She perched on
the edge of his bed as the boy drank thirstily.

'What's that flapping noise?' he enquired as he
handed back the empty beaker.

'It's only the plastic sheet Bob put over the hole in
the roof of the old wing.' To the child, sleeping in a
strange house, it probably sounded eerie, Jay realised
with sympathetic insight. Aloud she said practically, to
divert Tim's thoughts, 'There isn't a light switch in this
room, it's the old nursery suite. The switch is in my
room, next door.'

'What'll I do if I want . . .?'

'Call me, I'll hear you.' What with the rick sheet and the dangling rope, and the chaotic state of her own thoughts, she had had no sleep so far since she came to bed, and it was unlikely she would get any rest for the rest of the night, she acknowledged wearily. 'Tomorrow I'll buy you a torch when I go to town with your uncle,' she promised, conscious of the seven-year-old's need for independence. 'That way,' she added tactfully, 'you needn't risk bumping your toes again.'

'Can I have a red one?' Tim staked his claim with alacrity, and Jay smiled in the darkness.

'If I can find one,' she promised readily, 'and a spare battery as well.'

'Ooh, smashing!'

'Now go to sleep.' Satisfied that his mind would have other things to dwell on now rather than the noises from outside, Jay kissed the top of his head and tucked the blankets round him, and left him to dream of his promised new possession on the morrow.

'I wish I could get back to sleep so easily,' she thought enviously as she padded barefoot back to her own room. Her bed felt cold when she reached it. She had flung the sheets aside when she heard Tim call, and in her haste to find out what he wanted she had not bothered to pull the covers across again to preserve what warmth there was. The sheets struck chill, and she shivered as she climbed back between them and drew her wrap more closely about her, wishing she had accepted Martha's kindly offer of a hot water bottle.

'I like the comfort of a bottle myself, though Mr Lyle never bothers with one.'

Perhaps Lyle, too, regretted his refusal now. Jay's straining ears caught the sound of an opening door further along the landing from her own. Lyle's door. It closed, wood gentled against wood under a cautious hand, and a whisper of stockinged feet stole along the landing towards her door. Would they pause if Lyle knew she was awake? They went on, and began to descend the staircase. The hinge in the kitchen door creaked. A pause, and then the now

familiar soft thump as Lyle stamped his feet into
place inside rubber boots.

'I'm frequently out at night. . . .' What was it he had
said? 'Out on the sheepwalks, attending to the lambing
ewes.' Instinctively Jay glanced at her bedside clock.
The luminous hands stood at two-thirty. Her glance
strayed on, over to the window. She had pulled the
curtains back when she got into bed, and faint light
came through the glass square. She frowned in the
darkness. Water streamed down the pane, driven by the
wind. How long would Lyle have to remain out of
doors in the cold and the wet, she wondered, selflessly
denying himself rest in order to succour his flock in the
age-old ritual of spring? The fire had destroyed his sleep
as well as part of his house the night before, but still he
rose uncomplaining and went out into the streaming
darkness, putting the needs of the ewes before his own.
Suddenly Jay yearned to go with him, to share the cold
and the rain and the work, and share, too, the moment
of wonder that comes with the first weak bleat of a
newborn lamb. To hold the experience to her, as a
precious link between them.

For a brief moment she hesitated, but even if she
could have got dressed in time, and managed to catch
up with Lyle, there were Tim and Holly to consider.
They could not be left alone. In the cold, dark watches
of that restless night, Jay knew Lyle had been right to
refuse to house his niece and nephew, unless she herself
was willing to remain and look after them. Just as he
had been right in erecting the tarpaulin instead of
waiting for the scaffolders tomorrow. . . .

There were two lambs in separate baskets, one on
each side of the hearth, when Jay came down to
breakfast the next morning.

'Are they both orphans?' Jay's heart twisted in
sympathy for the frail-looking, woolly pair.

'No, there were two sets of triplets last night,' Martha
answered, busying herself at the stove. 'The ewes would
have been hard put to it to feed three each, so Mr Lyle
brought in the smallest one of each set. He thought Tim

and Holly might like to feed them, to give them an interest while they're cooped up in the house. He reckons it can't be much fun for them, not being able to go outside to play, and with the lambing and the fire and all, he can't spare the time to play with them himself.'

Lyle had shown no inclination to play with the children at all, but—was she being quite fair to him? Jay's conscience reproached her. It was less than forty-eight hours since she brought Tim and Holly to their uncle's house, and events since then happened at such a speed as hardly left time for play. It was unexpected consideration on Lyle's part to try to relieve the children's boredom, Jay conceded grudgingly. Perhaps after all he did not dislike the children. Only herself. . . .

'I'll go into the study and finish packing the rest of the estate records.'

'Breakfast won't be ready for half an hour yet,' Martha offered obligingly.

'That'll be time enough.' Jay escaped thankfully to the diversion of her work, but when the last volume was safely packed, and the lid of the salvage box shut, she escaped equally thankfully back to the warmth of the big kitchen.

Lyle was there before her.

'I've given the children their breakfast, Miss Jay. They couldn't wait to start on feeding the lambs,' Martha smiled indulgently, and added, 'Bring your porridge and eat it by the fire, you look fair frozen!' Her keen eyes had not missed Jay's uncontrollable shiver as she came into the room.

'I'm not cold,' she denied untruthfully, and Lyle sent her a quick glance and said,

'You'll be out in the cold if you remain at the table. I'm having my breakfast by the fire as well, to keep an eye on the feeding session.' He put his own bowl of porridge aside, and kneeled beside Holly. 'Do it this way.' Patiently he tilted her plump little arm higher. 'Hold the feeding bottle like that, and I'll hold the lamb for you, He's stronger than he looks, and if you're not careful he'll pull the teat away and blow milk all over you.' He smiled down at Holly, and the little girl smiled back, and he held the eagerly sucking lamb so that the child should have the pleasure of feeding it without the struggle of trying to control it. Watching the two from her seat on the other side of the hearth, Jay felt her eyes sting. This was no affectation on Lyle's part, to impress her. Indeed, it was plain he had forgotten all about her. His lean face was relaxed, his well cut lips curved upwards in a bow of genuine pleasure, and he and Holly were alike totally absorbed in tending the frail new life between them. Jay forced her porridge down a suddenly closed throat. This was just such a precious moment as she had longed for, for herself, last night.

'Come in, there's no need to stand on ceremony,' Martha called out as a brisk knock sounded on the outside door, and the senior scaffolder appeared and said to Jay,

'I got your note tacked on to the salvage box, that you wanted to see me about something, Miss Jay?'

'Oh, yes.' Jay dragged her mind back to what she had been doing before breakfast, and wondered wildly what it was she had wanted to see the man about.

'I know!' she exclaimed thankfully. 'It's my portfolio of cartoons on the Gulf contract. I'd like you to take it with you when you return to Chester, and give it to my father.'

'The guv'nor said you might want something bringing back,' the man nodded. 'I'll see he gets it,' he promised cheerfully, and added, 'We've got an early start this morning. The rain's cleared off, so we should be finished just after midday. The scaffolding and the corrugated iron sheets will protect what's left of the damaged rooms until work can be started on restoring them.' He picked up the portfolio from the table. 'I'll put this in the van right away, then I can't forget it. Unless there's something else you want, Miss Jay, I'll get along now and carry on with the erecting while it's still fine.'

'Nothing else, thanks,' Jay replied, but as her eyes

rested on Lyle and Holly with the lamb on the other side of the hearth, she had to fight down an insane desire to call the man back, and beg him to erect a scaffolding round her, to protect what was left of her heart.

CHAPTER FIVE

'HAVE you finished packing the volumes in the salvage boxes?' Holly's lamb drained its bottle of milk and lay contentedly sucking her fingers, and Lyle rose from his knees beside her.

'Yes, that's the lot. For the moment.' Jay gave him an oblique reminder that there would probably be others after the contents of the study had been sorted. 'They'll go back to Chester when the scaffolders return today.'

'If they're that badly scorched,' Martha commented in a puzzled voice, 'I can't see why you don't just drop them in the dustbin here. It seems silly, to me, to take rubbish all the way back to Chester to throw it away, even if you have got a contract to clear up the damage caused by the fire.'

'It isn't rubbish,' Jay protested, and her laugh in her own ears sounded forced. If Martha carried on in this vein, she might make Lyle reconsider his decision to have the estate records micro-filmed, and it had been difficult enough to convince him of the worth of that in the first place. 'It's all the records of the pedigree herd,' she threw in a reminder to Lyle of what he said the records were worth to him.

'I can't see what good records are, if you can't read them,' Martha argued stubbornly, and Jay felt she could have shaken the housekeeper for her persistence. She was as bad, in that respect, as Holly. 'Mr Lyle said the books was toasted to a crisp,' Martha said lugubriously, 'and you could scarce make out the writing on the pages.'

'So they are.' Jay controlled her patience with an effort. 'But there's a special filming process that can pick out lettering that's almost invisible to the human eye, and reproduce good, legible copies.'

'Humph!' Martha remained unimpressed by the marvels of modern science. 'If this film thing can pick out writing that's too faint for a body to see, let's hope it'll discover something written down somewhere that gives a clue as to the whereabouts of the Gaunt painting. By the time all the work's finished, and the Hall's been put to rights again,' she said pessimistically, 'Mr Lyle's going to need to sell one to pay for the other, it seems to me.'

'The Gaunt painting?' Jay raised enquiring eyebrows in Lyle's direction, intrigued in spite of herself. 'Beth told me quite a lot about the history of the Hall, but she didn't mention anything about a painting. If you've got one that's been damaged,' she added promptly, 'we can restore that for you as well.'

'Well spoken!' Lyle's eyes twinkled back at her. 'That shows good business acumen on your part,' he applauded, 'and I'm sorry to disappoint you, but there isn't a painting.'

'But Martha just said. . . .'

'I'll explain to you on the way to town,' Lyle cut her short. 'I've finished the milking, and you've packed your books.' They were not her books, but Jay let it pass, and tried to subdue an unexpected uprush of expectancy when he added, 'How soon can you be ready?'

'Ten minutes, to change and collect my cheque book,' she replied promptly, and could have flailed herself for being so transparent. She sounded like a gauche schoolgirl being offered an unexpected treat. Last night she had gone to bed dreading the coming journey into town with Lyle. This morning . . . 'I should have told him at least half an hour, and then kept him waiting,' she regretted, too late. She should have let him see it did not matter to her whether it was half an hour or two, but instead. . . .

'You can have ten minutes to change. You won't need your cheque book.' The twinkle left Lyle's eyes, and the more familiar steel appeared in its place.

Snubbed. Jay's brief pleasure in the prospect of the

outing vanished, and she flushed at the curtness of his tone. 'That's put me in my place,' she told herself ruefully, and avoiding his eye she said aloud, 'I won't be long,' and ran past him and up the stairs, her dread of the journey returning in full force. 'Lyle's as prickly as a hedgehog, and about as unpredictable!' she muttered edgily. She had spoken without thinking, still automatically assuming responsibility for the children, and in one brief sentence Lyle had left her in no doubt he considered the children his responsibility, and his expense. And herself the outsider.

'I'll buy Tim his torch. Lyle can't prevent me from giving him that,' she comforted herself. It was unreasonable to resent Lyle taking responsibility for the children, when less than twenty-four hours ago she had tried her hardest to make him do just that, but just the same his snub smarted, and she did not feel like being reasonable. With angry hands she tugged a black polo-necked sweater over her head and began to brush her hair with a fierceness that made her wince.

'Steady on,' she cautioned herself, 'it's your own head you've got under that brush, not Lyle's.' She put the brush down and picked up a gold rope necklet and fixed it round her throat to lighten the solid darkness of the sweater, but she left her oatmeal wool suit unadorned, adding only neat black patent leather court shoes and a handbag to match, and carrying her gloves, and exactly ten minutes later she presented herself to Lyle, with her confidence at least partly restored by the knowledge that she looked her best.

'I'm ready.' Nothing could make her ready to face the strain of the journey into town alone with Lyle, but she was as ready as she would ever be. Lyle was ready, too, and waiting for her. He gave her a quick, comprehensive glance as she rejoined him, and Jay's heart answered with an uncontrollable lurch. He looked unbearably handsome. She caught her lower lip between her teeth, and the small, sharp pain of it helped to steady her, and clear the daze from her eyes as she looked at him. His chocolate brown sports jacket and matching slacks were casual, but their tailoring was not. Both the material and the cut were of impeccable quality, and his cream shirt was pure silk. His finely woven wool tie picked out the flecks in the tweed of his jacket, and like herself he was hatless.

'Let's go.' He helped her up into the white Range Rover parked outside the door, and Jay sank back into the luxurious seat and pulled the seat-belt round her, fiddling with it in an effort to fill the silence between them. Her fingers tied the belt into knots of nervousness as Lyle slid behind the wheel and slammed the driver's door shut, and looked across at her ineffectual efforts.

'Can't you manage it?'

'I've got it twisted somehow.' Her voice came out curiously breathless. 'I won't bother with it.' In an agony of nervousness, she thrust it aside.

'You'll wear the seat-belt if you're riding with me,' Lyle answered her authoritatively, and leaned across the seat to help her. 'The harness straps may still be a bit stiff, they've never been used.' It was her own fingers that were stiff.

'From fright,' Jay silently scorned her own nervousness.

'I don't expect your Uncle Quintin ever carried any passengers.' She did not care whether the late owner of Millpool Hall had carried passengers or not, but she had to fix her mind on something—anything—to prevent it from reeling out of control as Lyle's hands reached round her, brushing against her own as he took the buckle of the seat-belt from her hold, and wove it back through the strap, untwisting it with deft fingers.

'Lift your hand over the strap.' His voice reached her through a mist, in which she was only conscious of the wild, erratic thumping of her own heart, a singing in her ears that held more of warning than of music, and the demoralising, breath-stopping closeness of Lyle as he leaned across her, the clean smell of good tweed from his jacket mingling with the faint, astringent smell of his after-shave lotion, that she recognised from when he first kissed her. His face was close above her own, close enough for their lips to meet. He only needed to turn his head. . . .

'Not that hand, this one.' His eyes were intent on unravelling the knots she had made in the seat-belt, and he did not turn his head. When she did not comply, he lifted her hand for her, and his touch jerked through her fingers like an electric bolt, shocking the mist aside.

'The Range Rover wasn't my uncle's vehicle.' He locked the seat-belt mechanism into place with a sharp click. 'It's my own,' he informed her casually. 'I brought it with me when I came from the South.'

And the seat-belt on the passenger side had never been used. The vehicle was not new, Jay noticed the registration letter when she rounded the Range Rover to reach the passenger side, and it proclaimed the vehicle as being two years old. Her heart suddenly ceased to thump, and started to sing instead, but it was a different singing from that which had afflicted her ears, and which now seemed to have disappeared.

'It doesn't mean anything,' she tried to tell herself desperately, aghast at the wave of relief that flooded over her on learning that the seat-belt had not been used before. It made her lips urge to accompany the music in her heart, and she pressed them together tightly, as if afraid they might burst into song of their own accord. An unused passenger seat-belt might simply mean—*must* mean, she tried to convince herself urgently—that for the last two years Lyle had carried singularly reckless passengers. Or passengers he had not cared enough about to insist on them wearing a seat-belt when they travelled with him? The thought came unbidden, and expanded. Surely if Lyle had carried a girl-friend in the Range Rover, he would have made sure she was safely buckled in before starting the engine? Or perhaps his girl-friend drove her own car? It was too much to expect that anyone so good-looking as Lyle had spent the last two years without feminine company, and he had insisted upon her, Jay, fastening the seat-belt before they started off. In her own case, Lyle had another reason for his concern, she warned

herself with ruthless honesty. While she was working
for him, in whatever capacity, he was responsible for
her safety, and she had just discovered to her cost that
Lyle took his responsibilities seriously. Just the
same ... her lips curved upwards at the memory, he
had insisted.

'Are you comfortable?'

If being torn apart by a bewildering mixture of love
and loathing, exhilaration and despair, tenderness and
resentment, was being comfortable, then she supposed
the answer must be,

'Yes, quite comfortable, thank you.' She sounded
rather like Holly, being polite, and Lyle's lips twisted,
but Jay was so busy looking out of the wide windscreen
in front of her, trying not to look at Lyle, that she did
not notice. Stonily she fixed her eyes ahead of her, all
the while agonisingly conscious of every slight
movement of him in the seat next to her. His hand
reached out, and his slender brown fingers closed over
the knob of the gear lever. Long, sensitive fingers, that
last night had eased new life into a cold and unfriendly
world, and looked as if they might be equally at home
fingering the strings of a violin.

'We'll slow down and let Bob take the herd through
the gate first.' Lyle braked to a crawl to allow the black
and white line of cows to amble through at their own
pace, on their way back to pasture.

'I'd rather watch them from inside the Range Rover
than from the top of the farmyard wall,' Jay remarked.
She did not attempt to hide the relief in her voice at her
present safe seat, and Lyle laughed.

'Once you get used to them, you'll lose your fear,' he
reassured her. 'You can't feel afraid of someone called
Daisy, can you?' he twinkled, and Jay forced herself to
smile back at him, but her lips, like her fingers, felt stiff.
She would not be at Millpool Hall long enough to get
used to the herd, let alone to learn which was Daisy and
which was not. For fear he should pursue his train of
thought to its heart-wrenching conclusion, she digressed
hastily.

'They're the wrong colour for the Hall. You should run a herd of Jerseys, to match the colour of the stone.'

'You reckon the Friesians would be a better match for the scenery around Chester than here?' he grinned.

'Perhaps you're right, but the herd's here to stay, so you'll have to be satisfied with sending their records to Chester instead.'

The herd was here to stay, but she was not. 'Talking of records . . .' They had talked of the herd for long enough, Jay decided uneasily. It skirted the edge of things she did not want to think about, let alone to discuss, particularly with Lyle. 'What was it Martha was saying, about a painting?' Paintings were a nice safe subject, and she pursued it with a kind of desperation. 'She seemed to think the micro-film process might pick up something on the estate records about . . . how did she put it?' she wrinkled her forehead, trying to remember.

'The Gaunt painting,' Lyle supplied for her, and to her surprise he threw back his head and gave vent to an amused chuckle. Jay stared at him in surprise. Away from his work he looked younger, almost carefree, as if he intended to make the most of the few stolen hours of leisure. In spite of herself she began to relax, and her lips curved in an answering smile that, this time, was not forced.

'*That* old tale!' Lyle exclaimed amusedly.

'Is that all it is, just a tale?' Jay asked, and her voice betrayed her disappointment.

'Sorry to disappoint you.' Lyle raised his hand to Bob as the farmhand held the gate open for them to pass through, and set the Range Rover rolling again. 'I was brought up on the story,' he laughed. 'I used to dream of unearthing buried treasure, and restoring the family fortunes. I was only young at the time, and realism has since prevailed,' he confessed with a rueful smile.

From the cut of his clothes, and his choice of transport, his fortunes could hardly have been in a parlous state to begin with, Jay thought drily, and tried

to close her mind to the other, engaging thought, of
Lyle as a young boy, dreaming.

'The tale's based on fact,' her companion went on,
unaware of the way her heart twisted as her mind
peeled away the wrappers of the years. 'Most of these
tales are, of course, but the legend that grew round this
one was probably just wishful thinking on the part of
some of my more impecunious ancestors.'

'Tell me,' Jay begged him, and added rather lamely,
'I love listening to stories.' She could sit and listen to
the sound of Lyle's voice forever, she thought wistfully,
and while it recounted the tales of yesteryears, it no
longer had the power to hurt.

'Once upon a time. . . .' Lyle smiled across at her. He
had a peculiarly sweet smile, Jay discovered with a
pang. The first one he had thrown in her direction.
She wondered, when they first met, if Lyle's smile was
capable of warming his eyes, like Beth's. Now, she saw
that it did, and the discovery gave her nothing but pain.

'Once upon a time, the squire of Millpool Hall had
his portrait painted.'

Jay did not mind his gentle raillery. There was no bite
to it, just a mild teasing, as if he was enjoying the story
as much as she.

'Go on,' she urged, and settled back in her seat with
her face averted. She would have liked to close her eyes,
the better to savour the sound of Lyle's voice, but she
had to listen to the story it told as well, in case he might
mention it to her later and wonder why she did not
remember the details of what he said.

'My ancestor, being a man of some substance,
engaged the most fashionable portrait painter of his day
to do the work,' Lyle continued easily, as if the story
was so much a part of him that it had become real life.
He brought it to life for Jay. 'In fact, he engaged the
court painter of Charles the First to do the work.' He
paused significantly, and added in a throw-away tone,
'None other than Sir Anthony van Dyck.'

'Who?' Jay's head jerked round, and she sat bolt
upright in her seat, her euphoria vanished. 'Did you say

van Dyck?' she demanded incredulously. 'You can't mean it? Surely, you're joking?'

'No joke,' Lyle assured her, his grin expressing his delight at the success of his bombshell. 'I told you, the legend is based on fact. We know that much is true from family documents.'

'But—a van Dyck!' breathed Jay in an awed tone.

'No less,' Lyle confirmed casually. 'I've actually got the bill for the work, in the estate records.'

'Not the records I sent to Chester?' Jay felt sick at the thought of such a priceless document being toasted to a crisp, as Martha so expressively described it.

'No, those volumes are Uncle Quintin's records, covering the estate since he took it over,' Lyle calmed her fears. 'The very old family papers are all in a locked deedbox in the study. It was the first thing I checked after the fire, and although the box itself is badly scorched, the contents are untouched. I'll show them to you,' he offered. 'You'll find them interesting.' He took her interest for granted, but Jay did not mind that, either. She *was* interested. Fascinated would be a better word. Her eager look begged him to continue.

'The initial cost of the portrait is almost unbelievable, when you reckon what would be its worth today.'

'It's almost unbelievable that a van Dyck could have disappeared without trace,' Jay exclaimed. 'Is there no record of what happened to it? Not even a hint, somewhere in the records?'

'Nothing,' Lyle shook his head. 'Only the record of it having existed in the first place, in the shape of the bill, which bears a receipt signed by the painter himself.'

'Then the bill itself is valuable.'

'Not nearly so valuable as an original van Dyck portrait would be,' Lyle pointed out drily.

'And in all those years, no one ever managed to discover where it had gone to?' It was almost unbelievable, Jay thought bemusedly.

'Not to date,' Lyle replied carelessly. 'I reckon every one of my predecessors for the last three hundred years has probably had a go at trying to find it, but if one of them succeeded, he was careful to leave no record of the fact.'

'Not even where they *thought* the painting might have gone to?' Jay persisted, and Lyle threw her an amused glance.

'Don't tell me the bug's bitten you as well?' he chuckled, and Jay felt herself go pink.

'I was only. . . .' she protested.

'No need to be prickly about it,' her companion laughed. 'The urge to unearth buried treasure has infected us all at some time, but even if you go over the Hall with a fine tooth-comb while you're doing your survey, I doubt if you'll come up with so much as a picture frame,' he predicted cheerfully. 'Remember, my family has had three hundred year's start on you,' he teased, and added more seriously, 'so don't let yourself get carried away by dreams.'

The dreams her errant heart were weaving were not about a lost painting, but about a lost cause. Her own. With an effort Jay dragged her mind back to what Lyle was saying.

'It's my belief the painting went the same way as the family silver at that time, to swell the Royalist funds during the Civil War,' he continued thoughtfully, and Jay's lips took on a bitter twist. That was not the lost cause she had in mind. 'The squire who had his portrait painted raised a troop under his own banner, and marched to the aid of Charles the First at Naseby, where his king lost his battle, and my ancestor lost his life,' he finished cryptically.

'And you think the painting . . .?'

'Was most likely sold off, to help to feed and arm his troop,' Lyle answered with conviction. 'Likewise the family silver, melted down in the same cause. The painting itself wouldn't be worth so much as the silver at the time, and since the only man who knew what really happened to it fell at Naseby, we're not likely to ever know its true end.'

'Perhaps your ancestor confided in his wife, and she may have kept a diary. Gentlewomen did, in those days,' Jay hazarded, determinedly fixing her thoughts on battles long ago, to prevent them from dwelling, painfully, on the battle she was fighting, and losing, within herself.

'No diary,' Lyle dashed her hopes with cheerful lack of concern. 'If local history's to be believed, Cromwell's troops based themselves for a time at the Hall, probably to rest after the battle, and when they eventually departed, the place was in such an impoverished state that the poor woman had better things to do than to keep diaries.'

'It was surprising that she and her family were allowed to remain at the Hall, after her husband had fought on the losing side.'

'When the occupying army had confiscated her jewellery, eaten the animals on the farm, and sacked the Hall of all its portable treasures, they probably thought the rest wasn't worth bothering about,' Lyle commented grimly. 'The place must have been virtually in ruins, and it was almost a hundred years later before the estate began to show signs of recovering its old prosperity.'

Lucky estate! Jay thought bitterly. It was unlikely her own heart would ever recover. Lyle had invaded it, robbed it of everything worth while, and like the occupying army of long ago, left her with a joyless, empty shell.

'Hello, it looks as if there might have been an accident farther along the road,' Lyle exclaimed, forgetting his story, and slowing down at the behest of the man who stood in the middle of the carriageway approaching a bend, and faced them with a 'stop' sign on a lollipop board in his hand.

'What's wrong?' Lyle asked through his opened driving window as they came abreast. 'Is there anything we can do to help?' Jay warmed to the 'we'. For a brief, exquisite moment, Lyle had linked her with himself.

'It's only a tree down across the road, on the other side of the bend, sir. The gangers are clearing it away now.'

So there was nothing they could do to help. The link snapped almost before it was forged, and guilt followed hard on the heels of sick disappointment. If there had been an accident, someone might have been hurt. Better to let the link snap.

'The carriageway's clear on the one side, sir. Just keep going, but slowly, until you can see round the bend.'

The man waved them on, and Lyle gentled the accelerator, and the fallen tree came into view, with a lorry drawn up beside it, and men busying themselves among the recumbent branches. The whine of a chain saw rent the air with a banshee wail.

'What a shame, to stand for so long, and then be felled in a moment, like that!' She knew how it felt. Lightning had struck her, too. Jay gave a glance of sympathy at the fallen giant as they passed it by.

'It's not the only one. There's another tree down, across the far field—look!'

It was too far away for them to see what kind of tree it was, and there were no leaves on it yet to give a clue. 'Will the gangers deal with that one as well?' Jay asked, more as a refuge from her own thoughts than from any real interest in the ultimate fate of the tree.

'No, that tree's on Nathan Wilson's land,' Lyle answered. 'He's my neighbour. He'll cope with it himself, I expect. It'll give him enough wood for log fires for next winter,' he added practically.

Log fires, and a wheelback chair drawn up to the hearth. . . . Jay gave herself a mental shake, and said,

'He's some distance away, to be a neighbour.' The farmhouse was only just coming into view across the fields.

'His land adjoins the Hall estate. You'd probably approve of his herd,' Lyle teased. 'They're Herefords—brown and cream. They match the stone of the buildings hereabouts better than my Friesians.'

The town, when they reached it, was mostly built from the same warm-coloured stone.

'It's quarried locally,' Lyle aswered Jay's interested query.

'Are the quarries still working?' The work at the Hall was a link between them, and Jay re-forged it quickly, conscious of the warmth flooding back. Conscious of the need for common ground between them. 'We might need some matching stone for refacing work, it'd be a help if we could find some locally.'

'The quarries are still working,' Lyle confirmed. 'If you need a supply of stone for the work on the Hall, I'll take you across to do your own haggling with the quarry manager.'

It was a concession to her professionalism that he did not say he would order the stone himself. A small concession, true, but Jay hugged the satisfaction of it to her along with the warmth as she slid out of the Range Rover on to the tarmac of the car park, and pulled on her gloves against the keen air.

'Where to first?' Lyle locked the vehicle doors, and joined her.

'You lead, I don't know the town.'

'Keep close to me,' he advised, and could not know how his words caught at her heart. 'It's market day, and it gets pretty crowded towards mid morning. If we get separated, make your way back to the pub cark park.' He turned her round so that she should identify the inn sign. The Roundhead. Even now, echoes of the Civil War and its aftermath still lingered. 'We'll have lunch here after we've finished shopping.'

'Lunch?' Jay betrayed her surprise. 'Aren't you in a hurry to get back?'

'Not until milking time this evening,' he answered easily. 'You might as well see something of the town while we're here, it's worth exploring.'

'He means while *I'm* here,' Jay rephrased drearily. Accepting that she would not be here for long. The brightness dimmed, and she turned to walk beside Lyle in depressed silence.

'You were right about the crowds.' Sturdy-looking housewives laden with shopping bags marched purposefully along the narrow pavements, and Jay ducked into a doorway for the third time to escape being jostled. 'Their menfolk ought to help them to carry those enormous bags,' she regarded a laden shopper with awe, and indignantly condemned the woman's absent husband.

'I expect her man will be at the market at this time in the morning,' Lyle replied acceptingly.

'Just the same. . . .' Jay rubbed a barked shin that had caught the full brunt of the swinging shopping bag, and felt disinclined to forgive the chauvinistic attitude of the local male population towards their burdened womenfolk.

'The men can't be in two places at once,' Lyle's tone accused her of being unreasonable, and Jay bridled at his implied criticism. 'I don't doubt they'll do their fair share of carrying the family shopping later, when the stock auction's over.' He drew her out of her doorway with a long arm, and kept it round her protectively. 'Walk in the roadway with me. It's closed to traffic on market days.'

'It's a wonder anything wider than a bicycle can get up it,' Jay retorted tartly, and added, wincing, 'And no cyclist in his senses would try to ride on this surface!' It was narrow, and roughly cobbled, an alley more than a roadway, and the eaves of the buildings on either side almost met above their heads, turning it into a tunnel.

'None of the locals try,' Lyle grinned at her expression, and tightened his grip round her waist, lifting her across the more uneven stretches as easily as if she had no more weight than a child. 'It isn't far now,' he encouraged her. 'Those big double doors just ahead of us are the entrance to the best store.'

His arm around her made her wish the alley would go on for ever, never mind the cobbles. The double doors were made of heavy glass, and swung open automatically as they walked towards them. A rush of warm air greeted them as they stepped inside, and Lyle dropped his arm from round Jay's waist, and a chill like that of midwinter froze her to the bone as he preceded her through the crowd towards a nearby escalator which bore the helpful notice, 'Ladies' fashions and children's wear—first floor.'

'The little ski suits are our warmest line, madam.' The assistant obviously took them for a married couple, and Jay regretted her gloves, and then felt contrarily thankful she had kept the left one on, otherwise goodness knows what conclusions the woman would draw from their purchases, she thought, growing hot at the obvious one.

'An ordinary anorak and corduroy overalls would serve the purpose just as well.' The ski suits might be the warmest line, but they were also the most expensive, Jay gave a surreptitious glance at the price tickets and winced at the figures marked up. The small suits were a dream, softly padded, and cosily cuffed at ankles and wrists, and they lay along the counter like vividly coloured birds, temptingly bright.

'The gay colours would be useful to locate the two imps when you want them.' Lyle did not share her reservations, and two ski suits were added to the pile of woolly jerseys and trews already stacked on the counter, a scarlet one for Tim, and a bright yellow one for Holly. 'If they go into hiding in the barn, they'll show up like lights on a Christmas tree,' Lyle chuckled, and nodded his agreement to the addition of Fair Isle cap, scarf and mitten sets to match. 'They'll need something for their feet that's warmer than the open sandals they're wearing now.'

'We can't get them shoes unless they try them on first,' Jay objected.

'Wellingtons.' The assistant produced her answer to their problem in the shape of brightly coloured rubber boots to match the suits. 'If they're a size larger than the shoes the children are wearing now, you can add lambswool inner soles and a pair of thick socks for warmth, and still be sure their toes have got enough room. Lucky children!' she exclaimed as she wrapped and taped. 'When are they going on holiday?'

'They're not,' Lyle answered, 'they're just back from the Gulf, and feeling the cold of England in March.'

'It must seem like the Arctic, to them, with this keen wind blowing,' the assistant was all sympathy as she passed Lyle the bill.

'It does,' Jay retorted feelingly, and hoped a portion of Lyle's outsize cheque would be paid as a bonus to their friendly helper.

'Is there anything you need to get yourself?' he enquired as he tucked the unwieldy bundle under his arm and bade farewell to the gratified assistant.

'Yes, I want. . . .'

'In that case,' Lyle did not wait to discover what it was Jay wanted, 'I'll take these back and lock them in the Range Rover, and meet you in the car park in about three-quarters of an hour,' he said briskly.

He acted as if he could not wait to get away. All the pleasure of their shared shopping vanished, and Jay felt sick. Lyle was no better than the men who went off to the stock auction and left their unfortunate women folk to carry huge bags of shopping back to the car park on their own. He had probably gone to join them. He was . . . Jay gritted her teeth, and only by a supreme effort of will managed to suppress the vitriolic descriptions that came tumbling into her mind, none of them complimentary to Lyle. Somehow she forced her voice to sound normal as she thanked the assistant for her help, and turned in Lyle's wake.

'He didn't even wait to ask if I could find my way back to the car park on my own,' she realised furiously, and knew she had no choice because Lyle and his parcel had already been swallowed up by the milling crowd in the store.

'It'll serve him right if I get lost, and keep him waiting,' she fumed. It was highly unlikely, as Lyle must have known. The main entrance to the store faced on to the cobbled alley, which itself led back to the car park of The Roundhead. For a brief, rebellious moment Jay felt tempted to enquire the times of the buses running back to Millford village, but reason prevailed, albeit reluctantly, as she remembered the dainty heels of her court shoes, and the long walk from the village back to the Hall.

'I'll be as long as I possibly can, getting Tim his torch,' she planned malevolently. But torches are not purchases that can be lingered over indefinitely, and she was soon the possessor of a parcel containing one red and one yellow torch to go with the ski suits, and two spare batteries, and still half an hour in which to do a ten-minute walk back to the car park. She remembered noticing a newsagents stall just inside the entrance doors to the store, and made her way towards it. 'I'll buy a magazine,' she decided, and took her time in making her choice from the display available, determined not to reach the car park before Lyle, and giving him the satisfaction of knowing he had kept her waiting. A very large lady was already engaging the attention of the assistant, trying to make up her mind about the purchase of a paperback novel, and Jay waited patiently, half shielded from the door by her fellow customer's bulk.

'Lyle!' She stared in surprise as he came through the glass doors, and strode towards the escalator. Jay frowned. He could not have gone to the market after all, as she supposed. Or perhaps—she glanced at her watch, and her frown deepened—perhaps he had meant to go, and then realised that the auctioneer would shortly be packing up for lunch, with the morning's business finished, and it would not be worth while to walk to the market, wherever it was, so he had opted to return to the store instead, and rejoin her there.

'If that's his intention, he'll be disappointed,' she muttered grimly. She would not be used as a stopgap for any man on earth, and that included Lyle. She kept her magazine in front of her face, and watched him covertly round the edge of the pages until the escalator bore him out of sight up to the first floor.

'Thank you.' She handed over her money with a bright smile, tucked her magazine under her arm, and slid out through the glass doors with as much haste as the crowd of shoppers would allow.

'It would serve Lyle right if I let him spend the rest of

the day looking for me,' she muttered unrepentantly, and without a backward glance she turned away from the store entrance in the opposite direction to that of the car park.

CHAPTER SIX

IT was exactly an hour from the time Lyle left her when Jay returned to the car park. She would have liked it to be much longer, but a growing emptiness inside her warned her of the long hours since breakfast time, and effectively destroyed any lingering rebellion, that had already begun to wane in the teeth of the icy wind.

'There's no need to overdo it,' she compromised. She had kept Lyle waiting for a full fifteen minutes over the stipulated time, which if her own temperature was anything to go by, should by now have ensured that he was frozen to the spot he was waiting on, she decided hopefully. She strolled nonchalantly on to the car park, and looked round.

Far from being frozen to the spot, Lyle was not there. Jay's temperature rose several degrees in a rush. 'I might have guessed!' she fumed, and then sudden panic cooled her angry thoughts. Lyle did not appear to be there, and she could not see the Range Rover, either. She could not remember exactly where they had left it. She had walked away from it with her thoughts occupied by the shopping, and left the problem of relocation to Lyle, but it could not have been far away from the inn sign. Lyle had turned her round to look at it, so that she could identify the place again. And now their transport was gone.

'He's gone back home and left me!' The fact that she had been tempted to do just that did not occur to her. She stood at the edge of the car park and clenched her fists, and did the same with her teeth to stop them from chattering, as cold as she had hoped Lyle might be, and rigid with anger against him.

'He's . . .' she choked.

'Here, Jay!'

She heard him shout, and saw the Range Rover at

the same time. A magazine appeared out of the driver's window, waving at the end of a long arm. 'I didn't notice you come, I got a bit carried away by an article in my magazine.' He flourished a copy of the *Farmers Weekly*, and Jay scowled at the inoffensive publication.

Lyle *should* have noticed her come. He should have been waiting for her, and shivering with cold in the process, and instead he was sitting warm and comfortable in the cab of the Range Rover, absorbed in an article about increasing the fertility of grazing land, totally unaware that she had kept him waiting. Jay seethed with silent resentment at his unawareness.

'I had to move the Range Rover to make way for a brewer's lorry.' So the Range Rover was not in the same place they had left it. The knowledge gave Jay no satisfaction. 'The driver wanted to get close up to the pub to make his delivery.' Lyle descended from the cab and locked the door, cheerfully oblivious of her indignation. 'Come and eat. You look absolutely frozen.' He slipped the ignition key into his pocket and took her by the elbow, and steered her in the direction of The Roundhead.

It was Lyle who should be frozen, not herself. She could hardly feel her feet and hands, and her face was stiff and numb, sufficient excuse for her silence as she walked beside him.

'I've reserved the table you ordered, Mr Gaunt. Over there, just where you said you wanted it,' the host beamed, and Jay relented slightly when she saw the table Lyle had reserved for them was beside a large and brightly glowing log fire. She held out her hands gratefully to the blaze, feeling life seep back into her face and limbs, aided a few minutes later by an ample bowl of thick, rich soup, followed by a delicious chicken curry that provided personal central heating par excellence, she thought appreciatively, and was almost ready to forgive Lyle by the time she had topped the main course with steamed ginger pudding, light and fluffy, and smothered with crusted cream, then turned her chair with a sigh of repletion to confront the fire, and toast her feet while she savoured scalding black coffee to finish.

'The Market Hall's worth a visit, and there's a fine view across the river from the edge of the town,' Lyle suggested when the meal was over, and at Jay's happy nod of acceptance he tucked her hand under his arm and took her to visit the Market Hall, then they made their way to the river, traversing more narrow, cobbled alleyways which housed the town's ancient two-storey shopping area that reminded Jay irresistibly of the familiar Rows in her native Chester, until they stood together, oblivious of the keen wind, absorbing the view from across the river.

'It's the same river that runs across Millpool Hall land, the one that used to power the mill.'

'Doesn't it now?' Jay did not care. She only wanted to listen to Lyle talking, to prolong this precious moment of togetherness, that once their work claimed them back at the Hall, would not come again.

'The mill's run by a generator now, helped along by wind power. Apparently during the summer months the river runs very low, and the power of the water isn't sufficient, so Uncle Quintin added wind sails to the mill, and what Martha calls a mechanical contrivance, to help things along,' he smiled. 'The mill isn't used for grinding corn any longer, only for generating electricity.'

'The mill pool's still there.' She tempted him to continue talking, clinging to the moment while she could.

'It isn't a natural pool, the river's damned just below the mill to keep up the level of the water, and direct a constant current through it when the river level drops, but it wasn't very efficient, apparently, which is why my uncle turned to wind sails and a generator. Between them, they supply the house and the outbuildings with all the electricity they can use, and he simply never bothered to drain the pool itself.'

'I thought generators were noisy things. I don't remember hearing it.'

'It isn't needed when the wind's blowing as hard as it is today,' Lyle told her, and added with a smile, 'If it's of any consolation to you, the wind that's freezing you half to death now is saving me quite a lot of money in diesel fuel!'

'I'm not cold,' she assured him truthfully. She was not. With Lyle's arm flung casually about her shoulders, protecting her from the crowds in the narrow alleys, and lifting her over the rougher stretches of cobbles, there was a warm glow inside her that had nothing to do with the food or the fire at The Roundhead.

It could not last, and even while it did, Jay knew it was madness to warm herself beside the fire of dreams, but she reached out nevertheless, as a little while ago she had reached out her hands to the glowing logs in The Roundhead, heedless that the fire of imagery might scorch and burn instead of warm, and leave her heart to perish in the icy aftermath once the transient glow had faded.

'We'll have to be on our way.' Lyle looked at his watch, and the glow faded as if he had clicked off a light switch. 'I must be home in time for the evening milking, and we've still got Martha's case to pick up from the village.'

Jay nearly asked him, 'What case?' and remembered just in time that to pick up Martha's case was the sole reason for their journey in the first place. She began to shiver uncontrollably.

'You're cold. I shouldn't have kept you standing by the river for so long.'

For ever would not have been nearly long enough, Jay thought mournfully, and shivered again.

'Let's run. It'll warm you up a bit before we start off.'

It was like running away from happiness. They reached the Range Rover breathless and laughing, but Jay's was a false laughter that only touched her lips, and she blamed the brightness of her eyes on the searching fingers of the wind, because it was pointless to blame her aching heart for the tears she dared not allow to fall in front of Lyle.

'Can you manage your seat-belt?'

'Yes, I think so, thanks.' She dared not risk Lyle
doing it for her. The memory of his closeness when he
had strapped her in before acted as a goad. If he should
lean across her again to reach for the belt clip, he could
not help but hear the agonised thudding of her misused
heart. It brought a pain into her throat and ears, and
made the delicate blue veining of her temples throb.

'I've managed.' The instinct of desperation forced her
shaking fingers to find the mechanism, and she clicked
the clip into place and leaned back with a sigh of pure
relief.

'The parcel of clothes for Tim and Holly is in the
back with the others.' She glanced round and saw
several more bulky parcels behind her. Lyle must have
done some shopping of his own when he discovered she
was gone from the store. He did not mention that he
had come back to look for her, neither did he ask her
where she had been, or what shopping she had done.
She tensed, waiting for his questions, and then relaxed
when she remembered the torches. If he asked, she had
an answer ready, and if it was not the whole truth, that
was her secret.

'The fallen tree's been cleared away.'

The road had been swept clean, but there were still
bits of bark and splinters of raw white wood scattered
in the grass of the roadside verge, all that was left
behind of a once magnificent tree. All that she would
leave behind at Millpool Hall were splinters of coloured
glass, patterned into a window, it was true, but splinters
just the same, that pierced her heart with the pain of a
coming separation not to be borne.

'Would you like to come in with me, and make
yourself known to the postmistress?' Lyle braked to a
halt in front of the tiny sub-post office which also did
duty as a grocer, greengrocer, sweet shop and
haberdashery store. 'This is where Martha stayed,' he
added as an explanation.

'Time's getting on,' Jay demurred. She did not
particularly want to meet the postmistress. There did

not seem to be any point in meeting the local people if she was to be here for only a short time. Depression settled on her like a cloud, and Lyle gave her a keen glance before conceding, 'Perhaps you're right, I don't want to be late back for the milking,' and disappeared inside the crowded shop to a loud clang from the spring door bell. He reappeared shortly afterwards carrying a suit case of a size that made Jay suspect, correctly, she afterwards discovered, that Martha had taken the minimum of belongings into her temporary accommodation, hoping, like Mr Micawber, that 'something would turn up' to take her back to her old suite of rooms at the Hall before very long. That something had been herself, and Jay flinched at the irony of ensuring the position of another woman in Lyle's home that she would give the earth to occupy herself.

'Eh, but these are lovely!' They spread out their purchases for Martha's inspection, and the housekeeper stroked the small garments with loving fingers.

'Can we try them on, Jay?'

'Can we go out to play, now?'

'Let Miss Jay and your uncle finish their cups of tea first.' Martha tried in vain to stem the eager barrage of questions, and Jay smiled indulgently.

'Why not? There's over an hour of daylight left yet. You'll work up an appetite for supper if you go out to play for a while now.' She pulled off cottons and popped on woollies as fast as was possible with the impatient wrigglings of five- and seven-years-old.

'Eh, they look right little pictures.' Martha surveyed the now cosily clad pair when Jay had finished. 'If only their mother could see them!'

'She will, in a few weeks' time.' Lyle put down his emptied cup and rose to his feet, and added with a grin, 'Though I doubt their outfits will be in quite the same mint condition as they are now by the time Beth returns!'

'The fabrics are all washable, and non-iron,' Jay hastened to reassure the housekeeper.

'They've got lovely big pockets.' Tim buried his small

fists deep into his latest discovery, uninterested in such mundane things as fabrics.

'Pockets ... that reminds me.' Jay opened the parcel she had brought for them, and produced the two torches. 'Here's something to put in your pockets.'

'A red one? You remembered!' Tim thanked her gleefully. 'I'll be able to see absolutely everywhere now, even in the middle of the night,' he gloated.

'The battery won't last long,' Lyle predicted amusedly.

'I've got some spares.' Jay smiled back at him, well pleased with the success of her gift.

'You never know, I might find the Gaunt painting. It might be hidden away somewhere, in the dark,' Tim planned hopefully.

'Don't start investigating on your own,' Jay began worriedly, and cast a reproachful look at Martha, who admitted guiltily,

'The laddie asked me, so I told him.'

'It's no good you going on a treasure hunt to find the long-lost painting,' Lyle dashed cold water on Tim's enthusiasm. 'That was sold to raise money to help the Royalists in the Civil War. Your ancestor raised a troop of men and marched out to battle beside his king.' His eloquent tones made the most of the drama for the boy's benefit. 'Didn't your daddy tell you?' he asked.

'No, he never said.' Tim's eyes were round with excitement and awe. 'Tell me now?' he begged, the painting clearly forgotten already.

'After supper, before you go to bed.' Somehow Jay knew Lyle would keep his promise to the child, without any prompting from Tim. 'I've got to help Bob with the milking as soon as I've changed out of these clothes. Everything has to wait until after the milking's done.' He turned towards the stairs with the caution, 'So don't risk poking about in dark corners for things that aren't there. All you're likely to find is a large spider.'

'Ugh!' Tim's shudder was genuine, and a wave of relief washed over Jay. She looked straight at Lyle, across the child's head, and her eyes flashed a message that said, 'Thank you.' She had not expected such insight from the boy's uncle. He was a man, and a bachelor, and could not be expected to share her forebodings, and until now he had not appeared to be overly concerned about his niece and nephew.

'Thank you.' The soft, deep violet of her eyes said it for her. That he read her message aright, Jay did not doubt. Momentarily, his eyes held her own, but they did not give her such easy access to his reply. She stared into them, forgetful of Tim and Holly and their bright new clothes, forgetful of Martha. Lost in the warm honey gold of his stare, that answered her—what?

Laughter was there. Or was it derision? Was he jeering at her for fussing too much over Tim? Or perhaps blaming her for providing the boy with his torch in the first place, a clear invitation for him to go poking about in dark corners. The softness in Jay's eyes fled, and an angry spark took its place. How could she possibly have known that Martha would tell Tim the story of the painting, filling his imagination with the details of the old legend? And now the damage was done, and the boy was caught by the spirit of adventure, how could Lyle jeer at her, Jay, for being concerned for Tim's safety? The boy was lively, imaginative, and at seven years old, unaware of what dangers might await his small person if he poked about in dark corners with his new torch. Lyle had just ensured, very neatly, that he would not. The answering spark that pushed away the laughter in his eyes reminded Jay sharply of the fact, and their two glances held and clashed with a ring of steel between them.

'I can hear Bob coming in with the herd.'

The now familiar, 'Goo-ern,' and a protesting bellow, floated into the fraught silence between them.

'I'll be with him in five minutes.'

Lyle turned away and took the stairs three agile steps at a time, and Jay blinked, released from the magnetism of his stare, and tried unsuccessfully to refocus her eyes on a room that, despite the presence of Martha and the two children, seemed suddenly empty.

'If we don't go outside now, it'll soon be too dark.' Suddenly it became necessary to escape the house before Lyle came downstairs again. 'Pull on your gloves, Tim, and put your torch in your pocket.' Jay performed the service for Holly, and handed her the inevitable teddy bear.

'Will you be warm enough yourself, Miss Jay?' Martha asked her concernedly.

'We shan't be outside for long, and I'll tie my scarf over my head.' Jay knotted the silk square under her chin, and challenged the children, 'Who's first out of the door?' The sound of Lyle's bedroom door closing overhead panicked her out of her chair and across the flagged floor, and ignoring Martha's look of surprise she bustled Holly and Tim outside, and closed the kitchen door behind her just as Lyle's footsteps began to descend the stairs.

'Just in time!' she breathed thankfully, and suggested aloud to the children, 'Let's explore the garden on the other side of the house.' It was farthest away from the milking sheds, and would make sure their paths did not cross with Lyle's.

'I'll race you there!' Nothing lost, Tim was off like the wind, and for once Jay was glad to follow him. She grasped Holly by the hand and ran, and despised herself for running away from Lyle.

'Let's play tag.' Tim raced round the old wing of the house and on to the lawns that fronted the windows of the dining hall and study, the shattered, glassless windows with the scaffolding rising like a metal skeleton in front of them, and above, the plastic rick sheet still flapping in the wind, and the corrugated iron covering above that.

'Jay's on,' Tim cried excitedly. 'Come on, Holly—run!' With squeals of delight the two children released their pent up energy, and Jay obligingly ran as fast as her court shoes and the rough winter grass of the lawn would allow, until, breathless and laughing, she leaned against one of the scaffolding poles and begged for mercy.

'Pax! I can't run another step. You're too fast for me,' she capitulated.

'I'll run even faster when I get my kite,' Tim boasted. 'Bob says the faster I run, the higher it'll fly, right up to the clouds.' He spun with his arms outstretched to show how his kite would soar.

'You'll need a long string on it, if you want to fly that high,' Jay laughed.

'Higher 'n higher,' Holly chanted, catching their mood, and spreading her arms in a fair imitation of her brother, although her chubby legs were unable to match his surefooted agility.

'Hold tight on to your teddy, Holly!' Jay's call of warning came too late. In her eagerness to spin as fast as Tim, the little girl lost her balance and stumbled, and the teddy bear flew from her flailing hands. It skimmed through the air like a fluffy yellow missile, and Jay groaned aloud as she watched it disappear between the rick sheet and the corrugated iron sheeting of the temporary roof.

'My teddy!' Holly let out an instant wail, in which Jay felt strongly tempted to join. Instead she said briskly, and with a confidence she did not feel,

'Don't cry, I'll rescue him for you. He can't have gone too far in between the rick sheet and the corrugated iron.' She knew she had no option but to recover the toy if she hoped to get Holly to sleep that night, though how to perform the rescue was another matter. She looked round her desperately. The scaffolding was unclimbable in its present form, it was no more than metal uprights supporting the temporary roof, with no walkways erected in between as yet.

'Shall I go and fetch Uncle Lyle?' Tim looked ready to fly off at his usual speed, and Jay checked him sharply.

'No, he's busy with the milking. I'll run one of these ladders against the wall, and climb up and fetch the teddy back myself.' Thankfully her eyes lighted on a line of wooden extending ladders which the scaffolders had left stacked against the house wall, and suiting action to her words she picked up the top one. It was

surprisingly heavy. She had watched the men lifting
them dozens of times, with seeming ease, and it galled
her that a mere ladder should defeat her own wiry
strength. She took a firm grasp on the uprights, and
heaved. The only alternative was to call for Lyle's help,
and she refused to lower her pride to seek his aid.

'Have I got it placed about where the teddy
disappeared?' She exerted all her strength and struggled
to straighten the ladder up against the wall, and peered
above her calculatingly.

'It needs to come a bit more this way.' Tim was
patently enjoying this fresh diversion. 'I'll climb up for
you,' he offered obligingly when she had set the ladder
to her liking.

'You'll do nothing of the kind,' Jay quelled him
instantly. 'I don't want to have to rescue you, as well as
Holly's teddy bear.' She put her foot on the first rung,
and felt thankful she was not afraid of heights. Her
work frequently took her up ladders that other people
erected for her, and then stood obligingly at the bottom
until she returned to terra firma. This time, she would
have to ascend without such security, and in court
shoes, she realised with a qualm. Her accustomed
footwear for such activity was lace-up shoes with
sponge rubber soles that gave her a grip like a limpet.
Her court shoes had leather soles that were as smooth
as glass, and slipped disconcertingly as she started to
mount the wooden rungs.

'I think. . . .' She hesitated. It would not take a
moment to run back into the house and change into her
other shoes. And then she caught sight of Holly's small
face watching her, crumpling with misery at the loss of
her beloved toy. In another moment she would begin to
scream, and Jay knew from past experience that
nothing except the safe return of her teddy bear would
silence her. The noise would alert Lyle and. . . . Jay
gritted her teeth and began to climb.

'Can you see him?' Tim called up to her interestedly.

'Yes, he's slid along the top of the rick sheet.' She
hoped her answer reassured Holly more than it did

herself. The plastic sheet dipped over the hole in the roof above the dining hall, and the slight slope of it had carried the toy farther across it than Jay bargained for. She considered the distance with a frown. The corrugated iron temporary roof was only about twelve inches above the plastic rick sheet, which did not leave her much room in which to manoeuvre. 'If I lean right over and wriggle in between the two, I'll just about manage to grab the bear,' she calculated. It was either that, or push the toy still farther in to where a tear in the rick sheet would allow it to drop through, and into the dining hall below.

Jay wished, not for the first time, that Holly would grow out of her fixation for her teddy bear, and instantly felt ashamed of her own impatience. Holly's phase had lasted so long, she suspected, because of Andrew's necessity to travel so much in the course of his work, and the toy provided the one stable thing in a frequently changing world for its small owner. Now Andrew and Beth were coming home to settle for a year or two, Holly would soon lose her need for her toy, but that did not help her own predicament now, Jay reflected ruefully.

A mere two rungs from the top of the ladder, she ducked under the corrugated iron sheeting, and wriggled her head and shoulders into the aperture between that and the rick sheet. There was very little to hold on to, she discovered with a qualm. The top of the ladder was by now below her, and that only left the wall of the house, which was covered by the plastic rick sheet, and only afforded an indifferent hand hold. The teddy bear lay more than an arm's length away from her.

'Provided I don't edge in any farther than my waist, I can't tip over,' Jay decided. She was not sure how much weight a rick sheet was capable of bearing. This one looked much used, and there was already a long tear in it, and she did not feel inclined to subject it to the weight of her own healthy, albeit slim personage, above what must be a clear twenty-foot drop into the dining hall below.

'Holly, come down. Jay'll be cross. Holly!' Tim's cry alerted her to the fact that all was not well on the ground below her.

'Holly, don't go any higher. Ja-a-y!'

Tim was not a boy to panic. The sheer, naked fear in his voice brought Jay out from the confined space with a haste that cracked the top of her head on the edge of the corrugated sheet above her, and nearly upset her balance on the ladder as she turned to look below her.

'Holly, go back this instant!' Jay's face went white. She had been so intent on locating the toy, she had not felt Holly start up the ladder below her. The little girl's face, as white as her own, peered up at her from at least half way up its length.

'Go back, there's a good girl.' It was of no use scolding, the child looked as frightened as she felt herself.

'I can't climb down,' Holly whimpered, and Jay's heart missed a beat.

'Come up and join me, then,' she coaxed, and tried to make her voice sound matter-of-fact, the while her mind raced. If she could coax Holly to climb up under her, she could perhaps hold on to the scaffolding for long enough to lift her feet free of the rungs to allow the child room until she could manage to grab her.

'I can't. I'm frightened!' Holly wailed, and burst into tears.

'I'll come up and fetch her.' Tim started towards the ladder, and Jay cried out sharply,

'No, don't! Stay where you are. If you try to force her down you'll both fall!'

Whether it was the unexpected authority in her voice, or the sense of what she said, Jay did not know, but she breathed a sigh of relief when Tim obeyed her, and remained at the foot of their high perch, looking up.

'Don't look down, Holly. You're quite safe so long as you stand still, just where you are.' Jay began to climb down towards the little girl. If Holly became upset she was usually sick, and the possibility turned Jay cold. If Holly should lean over the side of the ladder. . . . In her haste to get nearer to the child, Jay felt her foot slip on the smooth rung, and tensely she forced herself to a slower pace.

'Perhaps I can climb down over you.' If she had been wearing her working clothes of slacks and sponge-soled shoes, it would have been easy, but with smooth-soled court shoes, and wearing a tight skirt, it was inviting disaster to try. Holly was tall for her age, and with her chubby arms outstretched, clutching on to a rung above her, the child's length stretched out over an impossible stride for Jay in her present clothes. Likewise, she dared not attempt to swing underneath the ladder and come down beneath the little girl. Once again, the soles of her court shoes would not hold her from an inverted position, and if she shook the ladder by such a manoeuvre, Holly might panic and lose her grip. There was only one thing left for her to do.

'Lyle! Lyle!'

'Uncle Lyle!'

Jay raised her voice, and shouted along with Tim.

'What the . . .?' Lyle rounded the corner of the building at a run, and his eyes took in the situation at a glance.

'Stay where you are, Holly. I'll come up and get you.'

Jay envied him his calm. She herself felt just the reverse as Lyle checked his pace and deliberately walked the last few steps to the bottom of the ladder, and said quietly,

'Jay, climb up to the top of the ladder if you can. It's best not to have three of us leaning on the centre of it at the same time.' Holly was too far up the ladder for even Lyle's long arms to reach her, unless he climbed up himself, and the inference behind his words sent a quick shiver along Jay's spine. The ladder was of sturdy construction, but what if it snapped under the weight of three people? The wind cut through her fine wool suit, icily chill against the clammy perspiration of fear. It was strange how she had not noticed the bite of the wind when she was right on the top of the ladder before. With trembling limbs she began to climb, and

Lyle waited until she had resumed her former position before stepping on to the first rung himself. As he ascended, he began to talk, soothing the child with words as he climbed slowly so as not to unduly shake the ladder. Jay wanted to close her eyes. If Holly should turn round to answer him, before he got close enough. . . . She dared not look, and then she heard Lyle say,

'There, I've got my arm right round you now, so you can't fall.' Jay's knees went weak with relief, and put her in danger of doing just that herself. 'Slide your hands down the outside of the ladder, then bend your knee and feel below you for the rung further down. That's the way! That's how the scaffolders do it.' Coaxing, encouraging, never once showing any sign of haste or impatience, Lyle gentled the frightened child step by slow step to the ground. It seemed to take an age, and Jay's nerves felt ready to snap when he said at last, gently and without any hint of scolding in his voice,

'Now you're safe. Run along inside with Tim, and get ready for supper.'

'My teddy's still on the roof!'

A small finger pointed, and Lyle's face turned upwards, in Jay's direction.

'Then I'll go and fetch him back myself. He ought to know better than to climb about on the roof!' Incredibly the child's uncle witheld any censure from Holly, and managed to make it sound as if he would scold her teddy bear instead. Jay stared down at him with disbelieving eyes. This was a new side to Lyle, one she had caught a momentary glimpse of when they were buying the children their new clothes. Was it only a few short hours ago? It seemed like a lifetime, and she had not expected to see the glimpse again, let alone so soon.

'Ask Martha to have a soapy flannel ready for your bear when I bring him in,' Lyle smiled at Holly. 'He'll get his nice yellow suit all dusty, up there.' He urged the two children on their way and Jay watched incredulously as Holly scampered off happily enough with her brother. If she herself had tried to achieve the same result there would have been immediate tears and protests. She felt a momentary flash of what could only be described as jealousy, that Lyle seemed to have succeeded so easily where she knew she herself would undoubtedly have failed.

'Time enough to indulge in feelings when I'm safely down at ground level again.' Jay thrust the feeling aside. By now she had been on the ladder for a considerable time, and her whole body was beginning to go numb with the cold, adding to the danger of her high perch. She looked down at Lyle, and was assailed by a cold of a different kind as she saw the expression on his face, looking up at her. It was tight, and angry, and if he had refrained from shouting at Holly, it was clear he had no such reservations about herself. He spoke, and his tone made the icy blast of the wind seem kind by comparison.

'Now perhaps you'll come back to ground level yourself, and explain what brings you scrambling up ladders the moment my back's turned, and putting your own life at risk, to say nothing of those of the two children,' he demanded curtly.

CHAPTER SEVEN

HE made it sound as if she was indulging in a mischievous prank the moment he was out of sight. The sheer injustice of Lyle's attitude stung Jay, as well as the indignity of being spoken to in such a manner. He made her feel, deliberately she felt sure, as if she was no older, and a good deal less responsible, than Tim or Holly.

'Holly's teddy bear skimmed up on to the roof,' she began heatedly, defending her own subsequent action.

'By itself, no doubt,' Lyle retorted drily, and Jay flared,

'Yes, *all* by itself. Holly was pretending to be a kite. I suppose you *can* remember what it was like, to pretend to fly, when you were Holly's age?' Her disparaging look suggested that such an age for Lyle might be far too long ago for him to remember. 'The trouble was,' she rushed on quickly before he could answer, 'while Holly was spinning round she lost her balance, and her teddy bear skimmed out of her hand, and landed up here on the rick sheet.'

The sheer incongruity of arguing with Lyle from such a lofty height suddenly struck Jay full force. It was a unique experience, she realised, at least so far as she was concerned, to be able to throw her words down into his face, instead of having to crick her neck to look up at him. She savoured the experience, and discovered it was pleasurable. It gave her an uprush of courage.

'Which is what brings me scrambling about on ladders, as you put it,' she thrust back at him forcefully, 'to try to rescue Holly's toy rather than risk letting her scream herself sick just before bedtime.'

'There was no necessity for you to do either,' Lyle criticised her harshly. 'You could have called me.'

116

'You were busy milking. Everything has to wait until the milking's done, remember?' Deliberately she mimicked his own words, and saw his face tighten, but from her lofty height she did not care, and rushed on heedlessly, 'Besides, I didn't need you.' Oh, would that were true! her heart mourned, and brought a darkness to her eyes that made her clutch fearfully at the sides of the ladder. 'I'm used to climbing ladders every day in my work,' she managed to force out through teeth gritted as much with fear of falling as with defiance or cold.

'In town clothes?' he questioned disbelievingly.

'Clothes make no difference,' she lied, and added defiantly, 'which is why I intend to retrieve the bear while I'm up here.'

It was against her better judgment. If the task had been anything to do with her work she would never have contemplated such a step, dressed as she was at present, but her independent spirit writhed under Lyle's dictatorial manner, and she turned and took a deliberate step on to the top rung of the ladder.

'Jay!'

'Don't bellow at me, I'm not an army recruit!' she shouted back at Lyle angrily, and without a backward glance she thrust her head and shoulders into their former position in the aperture between the rick sheet and the corrugated iron. Her body as she bent felt curiously stiff. She had not realised how numb with cold she had become, and for a brief moment she hesitated.

'Jay, come down. Come down at once, I say!'

It was enough. Lyle's authoritative tone stiffened Jay's resolution, and gave her courage the extra boost it needed.

'And I say I won't!' she shouted back crossly. The teddy bear was tantalisingly close to her, a mere whisker away from her outstretched fingers. It lay beside the long tear in the rick sheet. If she could stretch just an inch or two further in, she could give it a push and it would tumble down into the dining hall below.

Doubtless it would need a wash afterwards, as Lyle
said, but a toy with a coating of soot was better than
Holly crying herself to sleep. 'Let Lyle shout if he wants
to,' she told herself grimly. Lyle did not have to cope
with the child himself. 'Now I've got this far, I might as
well be hanged for a sheep as for a lamb. Or is it a
bear?' Jay wondered with a ragged attempt at humour,
and stretched herself on tiptoe to try to reach that vital
extra two inches.

She had forgotten her court shoes. She did not feel
the first, slight slip, her feet were too cold to register
any minor sensation. The second slip made itself felt. In
one heart-stopping second, her first foot flew from its
precarious hold on the top rung of the ladder, and
unprepared as she was to bear the sudden double
weight, her second foot followed it, leaving Jay
helplessly suspended by nothing but the width of the
top of the house wall under her hips. Unevenly
balanced, she lurched forward heavily and felt her shoes
slip from her frozen feet. Briefly she had time to wonder
if one of them might hit Lyle on its way down, and then
there was not time to wonder anything any more,
except where she herself might land.

'Lyle! Help!'

With a wild cry Jay plunged forward, her hands and
arms outspread on the rick sheet, and bearing the full
downward thrust of her weight, and only her legs still
flailing on the other side of the wall preventing her from
tumbling headlong to follow Holly's toy.

Under the sudden pressure of Jay's hands, the rick
sheet dipped still further, and the teddy bear slid rapidly
towards the now ominous-looking tear in the plastic
sheet, which under Jay's horrified gaze seemed to run
towards her. A rush of warm air came up through the
widening hole. She closed her eyes against an upsurge
of panic, and opened them again to find the tear was
indeed running towards her. The sudden pressure was
all that was needed to enlarge the already considerable
rent, and even as she watched, the teddy bear glissaded
gracefully down the dipping plastic, and disappeared

through the hole. Jay felt sick as she watched it fall. Someone had been in the dining hall below and upended some of the smaller furniture on to the top of the long refectory table; she could see what looked like a veritable forest of wooden furniture legs pointing upwards from below her. The teddy bear bounced off one of them and landed on the floor with a tiny thump. Jay swallowed on a throat that felt suddenly parched. If she was to fall, she would not bounce off the furniture legs like the teddy bear, she would become impaled.

'Lyle!' she croaked, and was unaware that her voice came out as a wordless whisper. It was impossible for her to wriggle backwards, there was nothing on which she could press her hands to give herself the necessary leverage. The tear in the plastic sheet was already within a few inches of her fingertips, and the material under her was beginning to sag, threatening to disintegrate and remove the last slight support she had left. In the few seconds that it took for her terrified mind to register the danger, there was an ominous crackling sound from the sheet directly under her, and the tear raced across the ill-used material to the very edge.

'Lyle!' Jay's hands grasped frantically for a hold, and met only empty air. Helpless to help herself, she began to slip forward.

'Lie still, I've got you.'

Steel fingers closed round her one ankle, halting her precipitate slide. Other fingers gripped the back of her suit jacket. She heard the top of the ladder scrape a protest against the wall, and then the fingers loosed their hold of her ankle and appeared beside her, sliding along the top of the wall. Sliding under her, easing her cautiously backwards, away from the terror of the waiting forest of inverted furniture legs, away from the torn plastic, drawing her out from under the corrugated iron sheeting and into the blessed coldness of the wind outside. Jay drew in its icy restorative with a deep, shuddering breath.

'Let yourself go limp. I'm going to carry you down.'

'No, Lyle. Don't!' Her breath expelled itself in a sharp cry of fear. 'I can climb down myself. You mustn't. . . .'

He did. With an easy dexterity that took no account of her adult weight, he turned her to face him, grasped her behind the knees, and bent her over his shoulder in a classic fireman's lift.

'Lyle, let me up!' Jay let out a shrill cry of terror as her world suddenly inverted, and she found herself gazing down at the ground, that looked to be at least a hundred feet below. 'Lyle. . . .' Frantically she scrabbled with clutching hands, grasping at his clothing, his arms, trying to push herself upright again. 'Let me go!' Anger burned through her extremity of fear, and she beat on his shoulders with two small, clenched fists.

'Keep still!' Unbelievably he reached up one hard hand and gave her a sharp spank, and Jay sucked in a hissing breath of disbelief.

The indignity of it! She hated Lyle with a black hatred for subjecting her to such indignity. He had allowed Holly to walk down the ladder on her own feet, so why not herself? He had not even scolded Holly, let alone spanked her. A red mist of anger darkened Jay's sight, and made the faraway ground swim in front of her eyes.

'Don't struggle, or you'll land us both in a heap at the bottom.'

For a wild, dreadful moment, Jay felt she did not care. Anything, even that, would be better than submitting to such humiliation at Lyle's hands.

'You can't negotiate the ladder by yourself, it isn't safe. You've lost both your shoes, and your feet and legs feel too frozen to support you.'

Lyle should not know how her feet and legs felt. He should not. . . .

He took the first step down on to the rung below, and Jay's mind froze. In old-fashioned fiction, this was where the heroine swooned, she thought hysterically. In modern-day reality, it was impossible to faint when her head was hanging upside down, with every drop of blood in her body rushing in its direction, including any that the biting cold might have left in her numbed legs and feet.

An eternity later, Lyle stood her on the latter, and she gave a gasp of relief that became shortlived when he leaned her backwards against the sloping ladder, and with one hand grasping the struts on either side of her so that she could not escape, he demanded harshly,

'What in the name of sanity took you up a ladder in shoes like this?' With a swift, angry stoop he bent down and grasped one of her fallen court shoes, and waved it in front of her nose.

'There's nothing wrong with my shoes,' Jay began defiantly.

'The soles are as smooth as glass,' he contradicted her curtly. 'It's a wonder you managed to stand on them on terra firma, let alone on the narrow rungs of a ladder.'

'How do you know what the soles of my shoes are like?'

'I know because I picked up the one that hit me, on its way down,' he enlightened her grimly.

'So it *did* hit you?' Irrepressible mirth bubbled up in her, that her shoe had found its target.

'Fortunately for you,' Lyle retorted silkily, 'it only caught the edge of my sleeve.'

Her mirth died, extinguished by the icy anger in his glare. The knuckles of his lean brown fingers showed white with the force of his grip on the ladder on each side of her, as if, at one more false word, that grip would tighten to crush the helpless wood, and her along with it. Jay went white, and her eyes on Lyle's face grew wide and fearful, dark with apprehension of what her taunt might make him do. It was too late to regret her untimely laughter. It might yet be too late to avoid its catastrophic consequences.

'I did it to stop Holly from screaming,' she babbled desperately.

'I didn't hear her scream.'

'She soon would have done. She always does, if she misses her teddy bear for more than a minute or two.'

'It would have been better to let the child scream than to risk her life coming up the ladder after you.'

'How was I to know she'd start to climb up after me?' Jay defended herself indignantly. 'She was half way up the ladder before I even knew she'd started.'

'You should have taken precautions.'

'What precautions?' Jay demanded hotly. 'I've climbed ladders hundreds of times, and I've never had to take precautions against children before.'

'You've never put anything at the bottom of the ladder while you've been using it?' Lyle questioned her, and his voice was sharply critical, so that Jay flushed and retorted spiritedly,

'Nothing, except the workman who erected the ladder for me in the first place. What other precautions am I supposed to take?' she asked wrathfully.

'Commonsense ones, at least while you're working at Millpool Hall,' Lyle insisted curtly, and Jay flinched at the 'while' as if he had struck her with a whip.

'While you're working here, you won't have a workman to stand guard at the bottom of your ladder, and since Holly and Tim will be playing outside now they've got their new clothes, I don't intend them to be put to any unnecessary risk through your carelessness,' he told her bluntly. He said nothing about the risk to herself. Presumably that was of no consequence to him.

'I'll supply you with a piece of wood to tie on the bottom of your ladder.' He silenced her protesting, 'But. . . .' with an imperious wave of his hand, and went on, 'The wood will be the width of the ladder, and reach up to the third rung. With that securely fixed to the struts, neither of the children will be able to stretch up far enough to reach the first available step. Your own legs are long enough to make the stride easily enough.' His tone said he did not care if they were not, she would have to manage somehow, and that by herself.

'With a piece of wood of that size fixed to the bottom of one of these ladders, it'll be unliftable so far as I'm concerned,' Jay retorted flatly. 'They feel like a ton weight as it is.' She refused to acknowledge the sense of such a suggestion. She refused to admit anything to Lyle, she told herself furiously.

'You won't be working with these ladders, you'll have an aluminium one, and I'll cut a piece of plywood to fit on to it, that'll not add to the weight much.'

'The scaffolders didn't bring my usual set of aluminium ladders. They came straight here off another job, and didn't know I'd be wanting my own equipment.'

'So they told me,' Lyle cut in briefly, 'which is why I bought a set of lightweight ladders when we were in town this afternoon.'

It was tantamount to dictating to her what equipment she must use in her work on the Hall. It was sheer high-handedness on Lyle's part, and Jay's snapping eyes expressed her resentment at such interference.

'You've thought of everything, haven't you?' Her voice was heavily loaded with sarcasm.

'Someone had to,' he retorted meaningly. Which meant she should have done, and had not. Before Jay could draw breath to answer, Lyle added, 'I'll fix the plywood to the bottom of the ladders myself before you start to use them tomorrow. I've already put my home in jeopardy once on your behalf, and now I've wasted almost the entire milking period rescuing you from what's left of the roof.'

'If I'm such a liability, why did you bother?' Jay flung back at him angrily. 'And as for your aluminium ladders, you can deduct the cost of them from our final bill,' she taunted him rashly.

'That won't be necessary, you can pay for them now,' he grated, and with a sharp movement that caught Jay unawares, his hands released the ladder on either side of her. She was free! Swiftly she turned to seize her opportunity, to duck away under Lyle's arm, but he was quicker than she. Even as she spun away from him, his hands came up and caught her, and turned her back again, his fingers like manacles round her upper arms, pulling her roughly against him. She flung back her head, shrill words of protest surging to her tongue, but with angry force his lips clamped down upon her own, stifling them unuttered.

He took his time about exacting payment; for rescuing her from the fire, and from the roof; for the cost of the new ladders. With deadly deliberation, Lyle claimed the price in full. He showed no haste, and no mercy. Cold as she already was, Jay felt herself go colder still, numb with the icy anger of his kiss. Her lips were ravaged and bloodless under the pitiless pressure, her eyes stricken pools of violet in her ashen face, begging him to stop. In a daze of despair she felt her senses begin to slip, and her body went pliant in his arms. Only then, when he felt her limp submission, did his fury finally spend its force, and with a quick movement of rejection he thrust her from him.

'I hate you. I hate you!' Her breath came in deep, gasping sobs and she swayed away from him, summoning up the last of her remaining strength to prevent herself from falling. 'I hate you. . . .' But Lyle was not listening, he had already turned away from her to grasp the ladder, and commanded her shortly over his indifferent shoulder,

'Put your shoes on, and go and pick up Holly's teddy bear from the dining hall, while I put the ladder back with the others against the wall.'

Instinct guided her feet into her shoes, and steered them towards the corner of the building, groping for the path that her blurred eyes could no longer see. Lawn grass gave way to crazy paving, and she followed it blindly, stumbling in her haste to get away before Lyle should replace the ladder, and follow her. She glanced back over her shoulder. He was in the act of lifting the ladder away from the wall, and lowering it to a horizontal position ready to stack it with the others, swinging it easily in his hand as if it was no more than a toy. He did not look round, and Jay averted her head and hurried on, and gave a gasp of relief when the corner of the house hid him from her view, cutting her

off from the shame of her ignominious descent from the
roof, and the searing humiliation of his kiss. She would
never forgive him for that kiss, she vowed. Never! It
was despicable. Cowardly. It was.... She ducked
hurriedly through an end doorway as Bob made his
appearance at the other side of the yard. She did not
feel capable of facing anyone, not even the amiable
farmhand, until she had regained her self-control.

Movement brought feeling back into her frozen
limbs, and some measure of warmth. Warmth met her
as she opened the door of the dining hall, and she
stopped just inside, memory flooding back. Warm air
had risen to greet her through the tear in the rick sheet.
She had assumed at the time that it only felt warm in
contrast with the outside temperature. She raised her
eyes, and saw the tear was directly above where she
stood. She looked away again, quickly, with a queasy
feeling in the pit of her stomach. If Lyle had not caught
her when he did, this was about the spot where she
would have landed when she fell. That is, if she had
missed the upturned furniture legs on the way down. She
swallowed, and forced herself to concentrate on the
warm air. It was artificially inspired, and she looked
round for its source.

A mobile gas heater? She walked slowly towards it,
her mind registering its pristine newness. Her foot
touched something soft, and she bent mechanically to
pick up the toy bear, her fingers making an automatic
brushing motion across the yellow fur. They went still
as her surprised eyes saw that the toy was unmarked.
The floor under her feet was freshly clean. So too, she
noticed, was the furniture. The reason for the smaller
pieces being upended on the top of the refectory table
dawned upon her. The room had been thoroughly
cleaned while she and Lyle were out. Or before they
went, she had no means of telling which. Her work that
morning had been confined to the study, and she had
not entered the dining hall since the insurance assessor's
inspection of the day before. Wonderingly she walked
towards the window. Another sheet of plastic, of a

thinner texture than the rick sheet, covered the erstwhile gaping holes in the leaded lights, allowing light to penetrate, but keeping out the searching wind. No wonder the air in the room was warm! A thought struck her.

The pieces of stained glass! The precious, irreplaceable pieces, that had fallen from the picture window on to the floor below. And now were not there. She gazed at the newly swept floor in shocked disbelief, through which she became aware of Lyle's voice speaking from just behind her.

'The temperature's risen nicely in here,' he remarked in a satisfied tone.

Jay's own temperature rose to rival that of the mobile gas heater as she contemplated the possible fate of the precious pieces of stained glass. The unthinkable clang of a dustbin lid echoed in her imagination, and she spun to face Lyle with every vestige of fear vanished under the onslaught of this unlooked-for emergency.

'The pieces of stained glass,' she stormed at him accusingly. 'Someone's cleaned the room, and they've carefully cleared away every last sliver of glass as well!' Even now she could hardly believe it had happened. 'How could you allow it to happen?' she demanded angrily. 'You must have heard me tell the assessor yesterday that I wanted to salvage every tiny piece of the bits that had broken from the window. It's the original glass, and it's absolutely irreplaceable!' Fury, and disbelief that anyone could be so careless as to throw away such precious pieces of history, choked her into momentary silence. Pearls before swine was an inadequate description, she told herself wrathfully. Sheer wanton vandalism came nearer to the mark!

'What day is your dustbin emptied?' she wanted to know urgently, grasping at the last frail hope of recovering the bits of glass. If the dustbin had not yet been emptied, it would be Lyle, and not she, who would sort through the rubbish, she determined vengefully.

'This morning,' Lyle answered her question indifferently.

'Then it's too late.' Her last hope gone, Jay turned her wrath on the person she held responsible, even if he was not the actual culprit. 'For two pins I'd withdraw from the contract!' she threatened furiously. 'What's the point of restoring a priceless stained glass window for an owner who cares so little about it that he allows someone to throw away the very material that no amount of present-day skill can replace. I suppose it's a case of easy come, easy go,' she accused him scathingly. She was being unjust, Beth had told her how much Lyle valued his inheritance, but she felt too upset to care. This further, unnecessary loss to the already damaged window was too great to be borne calmly. 'You had the effrontery to accuse me of not thinking,' she blazed at him, 'and yet you allow this. . . .' Her sweeping gesture included the spotless floor, the denuded window, and his own infuriatingly unruffled expression. 'And you don't even care!' she shouted at him incredulously

'I cared enough to do the cleaning up myself,' he countered in a brittle voice, and Jay stared at him, stunned.

'You cleaned the floor yourself? *You* disposed of the pieces of glass?' It was bad enough to think that Lyle had allowed one of his employees to perpetrate such a crime. For him to calmly admit he had thrown away the glass with his own hands was stretching credulity too far. 'You heard me tell the insurance assessor . . . you were there when I said. . . .' she stammered her disbelief.

'Which is why I cleaned the room myself, and went over every inch of it with a fine toothcomb to make sure each sliver of glass was rescued, no matter how tiny.' He reached down a long arm and jerked open the lid of a salvage box that lay underneath the refectory table. Jay had seen the box there, but assumed one of the scaffolders had left it for her, and so had ignored its presence in the room.

'There's your stained glass,' Lyle gritted. 'That's all I could find of it.'

'It . . . I. . . .' Jay ground to a halt. There, inside the salvage box, carefully spaced out on a roll of clean white wadding, lay the pieces of stained glass, of all shapes and sizes, some broken, some not, winking up at her derisively in half a dozen rich hues. 'There's more of it than I thought,' she blurted out the first words that came into her head. She could not bring herself to utter the ones she knew she should speak, like, 'I'm sorry,' or, 'Thank you.'

'That's because I removed the loose pieces of glass that were still hanging in the window, while I was about it,' Lyle returned crisply. 'The scaffolders said it would be another twenty-four hours before they could bring your equipment along, and I guessed that included protective gloves for such a job as this?' He raised an enquiring eyebrow in Jay's direction, and she nodded dumbly, unable to speak. 'You certainly need a stout pair of gloves for that kind of work,' he went on feelingly. 'Some of the broken bits had an edge on them like a razor!'

'Did you cut yourself?' Fear brought back Jay's voice. Without stopping to think she caught at Lyle's hands, turning them over in her own, frantically searching for signs of a cut. 'You shouldn't have taken the risk,' she cried anxiously. 'The glass segments are held together by lead, and it can be deadly.' If Lyle had sustained a cut, and the wound turned septic, it would be her fault. Remorse caught her by the throat. Lyle had done this to help her, just as he had bought the ladders, and, she was certain, the mobile gas heaters as well, because he had noticed how she suffered from the unaccustomed cold. And instead of thanking him, she had railed at him, resenting what she took to be high-handed interference in her work, when all the time....

'Lyle, I'm sorry.' It was out now, and she did not care, her pride was swept away in her agony to make amends, and she clung to his hands, her eyes beseeching his forgiveness.

'What for?' he asked her lightly, and disentangling his fingers from her own he reached down and closed the lid of the salvage box with a snap. 'I didn't cut myself. I used a piece of rag to handle the glass, and I suggest you do the same until your equipment arrives from Chester,' he advised practically, and added, 'By that time the rooms should have dried out completely. I bought the most powerful mobile heaters I could find, to dry the place quickly, so the work wouldn't be held up.'

He had not bought them out of a consideration for her comfort, as she supposed. Jay's hands dropped to her sides, and a black sense of desolation swept over her as Lyle added,

'Let's go and find Holly and return her teddy bear, before she starts to pester Martha.'

'Well, I must say, he doesn't look in need of a soapy flannel.' The housekeeper cast a critical glance at the unexpectedly clean bear. 'Though I can't say the same for Miss Jay,' she added. 'Dearie me, just look at your nice suit!' She clicked her tongue in disapproval. 'It's badly smudged on both the sleeves.'

That was where she had reached in under the corrugated iron sheets. Jay gave her sleeves a perfunctory glance and answered offhandedly, 'It'll brush off, it's a good-tempered outfit.' The same could not be said for the suit's owner, she acknowledged to herself edgily. Tension, cold, and the emotional seesawing of a fraught day, were beginning to take their toll, and she felt exhausted and irritable, like elastic that has been over-stretched for too long, and suddenly snaps.

'I'll go upstairs and have a quick wash before supper,' she decided. The brief respite would give her time to steady the seesaw, and gain some semblance of poise before facing Lyle again.

'I'm serving supper in the breakfast room, Miss Jay, like I said this morning,' Martha told her. 'Just until the dining hall's been put to rights again.'

Jay wished the housekeeper had not acted with such celerity. She washed and dried, brushed and combed, and slipped on a softly pleated dress that matched the colour of her eyes, and tried in vain to slow the speeding minutes before she must join Lyle at the supper table, with only the company of the children to act as a buffer between them. And that not for long, she realised with a qualm. It would soon be bedtime for Holly and Tim, and then....

'I'll put the children to bed myself, and remain upstairs with them,' she determined. In her present frame of mind, the prospect of Lyle's sole company for the rest of the evening was not to be borne, but the children offered a plausible escape route, and comforted by the thought, she went downstairs with renewed confidence. Voices came from the open door of the breakfast room.

'They'd cleared away the tree at the roadside by the time we returned, but there was another one fallen, back in the fields.'

Lyle and the children were already there, and Martha was settling Tim and Holly into their places, while their uncle was evidently regaling his housekeeper with the events of the morning.

'Was it one of our trees?' Martha tucked a napkin under Holly's chin with an expert hand.

'No, it was one of the stand of old trees lying back from the road, on Nathan Wilson's holding.'

'Eh, that reminds me....' Martha completed the tucking, and reached for a large tureen and started to serve the soup. 'I intended to give young Mrs Wilson my recipe for gooseberry jelly, and now I shan't be going to the W.I. meeting this week.'

'Don't miss your meeting on the children's account, Martha. I'll look after them for you for one afternoon,' Jay felt obliged to offer, and the housekeeper smiled.

'The meeting's not really in my line this time,' she explained with a twinkle. 'They've had to change the guest speaker at the last minute, because the one who was booked to come and talk about patchwork quilting has been taken ill. The woman who's replacing her is going to talk about make-up and hair-do's,' she explained drily, her own well scrubbed cheeks and nononsense bun silent witnesses to her own lack of interest in such frivolity.

'I'll deliver your recipe for you, if you like,' Lyle offered. 'I promised to go to see Nathan during the next couple of days. We need to get this stretch of the river dredged where it crosses my land, and his. It's silted up quite badly, and as soon as the spring work's eased a little, it'll pay us to get the job in hand as soon as possible.' He held Jay's chair out for her, and she took it silently, and saw with a qualm of misgiving that it brought her opposite to the only other vacant space at the table. Lyle occupied it as Martha closed the door behind her, and Jay hurriedly busied herself with her soup, regretting the diversions of the more populous kitchen, uneasily conscious of the silent tensions flowing between herself and Lyle across the smaller, more intimate board, their expression suppressed only by the presence of the two children.

Neither Tim nor Holly needed help to eat their soup, and Jay began to feel as if her whole world consisted of her own bowlful of opaque brown liquid, from which she dared not venture to raise her eyes in case they should encounter Lyle's across the speaking silence that not all the children's inconsequential chatter could break.

Martha released her at last when she returned with the second course, and Jay turned gratefully to help Holly to cut her meat, thankful for any occupation other than trying to swallow her own unwanted supper.

'I'll help you to clear away.' She rose as Martha reappeared with the coffee, but the housekeeper laid the tray on a table beside the fire and refused her offer firmly.

'There's no need, Miss Jay. The girl from the village will be starting work here in the morning, and the supper things will give her a job to do to settle her in. Be mother,' she suggested with a smiling nod towards the coffee tray, and Jay's heart gave a twist at the irony of the cosy, domestic scene, with the laden tray at her elbow on one side of the hearth, and the two children listening raptly to Lyle's promised story on the other. For once, Holly deserted her teddy bear and crept on to

CHAPTER EIGHT

'DRAT the phone!'

'I'll answer it for you, Martha.'

'Would you, Miss Jay?' The housekeeper cast her a grateful look. 'I've got my hands full with this tray.'

Jay smiled as she picked up the receiver, and Martha disappeared hurriedly kitchenwards with the after-breakfast debris, that made a perfect excuse for her to ignore the shrill summons of her least favourite household implement.

'Millpool Hall.' How easily it ran off her tongue, with a warm familiarity that might deceive her listener, but could not deceive herself.

'It's Nathan Wilson here,' the caller identified himself as Lyle's neighbour. 'I'd like to speak to Lyle, please.'

'The last I saw of him, he was heading towards the other side of the yard. I'll go and see if I can find him for you,' Jay offered reluctantly.

'No, don't do that, it'll be quicker if you give him a message.' The caller was evidently in a hurry.

'Go ahead,' Jay invited, and he went on in urgent tones,

'Lyle said he intended to come over and see me about de-silting the river.'

'Yes, I know, he mentioned it at supper last night.'

'Tell him not to come,' the voice was adamant. 'Tell him my stockman has just come in and reported a cow down. He says it's blowing, and off its feed. The vet's on his way now. Lyle will understand.'

'It's more than I do,' Jay thought, but promised aloud, 'I'll tell him,' and felt thankful that the message was short enough to remember, if not to comprehend. The phone receiver clicked down at the other end before she replaced her own. He *was* in a hurry, she shrugged. Apparently Millpool Hall was not the only

house to suffer from problems. She strolled across the
hall to the kitchen door and told the grateful Martha,

'It was Nathan Wilson, for Lyle. I'll go and give him
the message myself, if you like.' It was obvious that
Martha did like. The housekeeper was in the throes of
clearing away the breakfast things, preparing bottles for
Tim and Holly to feed the lambs, and instructing her
new help from the village on where to find this and that
in the kitchen cupboards, and was patently not free to
take messages. The new girl looked competent, if rather
young, and rejoiced in the name of Deirdre, and after a
smiling 'hello' Jay shut the door on the scene of busy
activity, and went in search of Lyle.

'He's in the barn, Miss Jay. I'm just going there
myself.'

'In that case, there's no need for me to go as well,
Bob, if you'll give him a message.' Jay grasped the
unexpected opportunity and recounted the details of
Nathan Wilson's early morning call.

'Aye, I'll tell him, right away, miss. I'll go and search
him out now.' Bob nodded unsmilingly, and left her at
a shambling trot, and Jay watched him go with a feeling
of surprise. Even at his most helpful, she had not seen
Bob hurry before. He always walked at the same steady,
deliberate pace, and he never spoke to her without a
pleasant smile.

'The cattle seem to arouse more emotions in the men
hereabouts than anything or anybody else,' Jay
muttered caustically, and turned away with a shrug to
collect her sketch book and measuring tape.

'I'll be working in the dining hall if I'm wanted,
Martha,' she located herself to the occupants of the
kitchen, and escaped thankfully to the blessed solitude
of her own work.

Warmth still emerged from the mobile gas heater,
although after the cosy kitchen the room did not seem
nearly so warm as it did yesterday in contrast to the
outer air. Nevertheless, the heater had done an excellent
job, Jay approved, running her fingers experimentally
over the newly cleaned furniture. The surfaces were dry,

although one or two places were badly scorched. One end of the refectory table was charred where part of the blazing roof had fallen in on top of it, and she examined the place closely. The flames had bitten deeply into the ornate carving of the leg, and she circled the table slowly, to discover the other legs were carved to an identical pattern.

'We'll carve another piece of oak to match, and soon have you looking as good as new,' she promised the table with a comforting pat, and turned her attention to the stained glass window. There, too, she saw thankfully, the remains left by the fire were sufficient to give her plenty of guidance to enable her to make a scale drawing of the window as it had been, aided by the replicas of the Gaunt coat of arms on papers in the deedbox which Lyle had brought for her to see the evening before. It had been a strange and unexpected evening. It started by her frantically seeking an excuse, any excuse, to quit the room when the children went to bed. Anything rather than be left alone with Lyle. It ended by her wishing that it might go on forever, with just herself and Lyle, and the wistful magic of the firelit room. Martha frustrated her plan to put the children to bed herself and remain upstairs with them afterwards.

'I reckon that's my treat at the end of the day,' she coaxed. 'It's many a year since I had the chance to tell a child a bedtime story.'

Faced with the glow of anticipation on the apple-cheeked countenance, Jay could not deny the older woman her simple pleasure, while her mind darted here and there, seeking another excuse to flee the room at the same time as Martha and the children. No matter that she railed at herself for being a coward, her heart was not equal to another contest with Lyle so soon after the last, that had it reeling still. Unexpectedly it was Martha who rescued her.

'The herd says to tell you, Mr Lyle, he's not too happy with the condition of that old ewe. He wondered if you'd stop by and have a look at her when you do your last rounds tonight.'

'I'll go now.' Lyle did not wait for his customary round of the outbuildings before he retired for the night. He rose instantly, as if he, too, might have been seeking an excuse to leave the room rather than be left in her company, Jay thought with a sudden catch to her breath. Contrarily she burned with resentment at the implied slight, ignoring the fact that it was only a reversal of what she herself intended, just moments before.

'Carry me upstairs, Uncle Lyle?' Holly begged with upstretched arms.

'You're much too heavy, after eating all that supper!'

He carried her, nevertheless, high on his shoulders, and Jay gave Martha the teddy bear to take along with her, feeling as forlorn as the forgotten toy when the breakfast room door closed behind the laughing group, and she was left alone. Contrary to her expectations, she could not settle down after Lyle left. The silent room brought her no peace, and she prowled round it, restless and uneasy, looking at a picture here, examining an ornament there. Lyle had not been at the Hall for long enough yet to leave the stamp of his personality upon any room except his own, and this room had only been reopened for use today. It still had a bare, slightly bewildered look, as of being awakened from a long sleep. It needed people, Jay thought, and flowers. Tomorrow she would search the garden for some early blooms to brighten the neglected room.

She returned to her chair, feeling better for the decision. She could relax in the knowledge that Lyle would probably be with the stock for some time, and the fire drew her, calming her restlessness, and soothing the uneasy turmoil of her thoughts. Lyle's magazine lay on the seat of his chair, but she made no attempt to pick it up and look at it. Her own magazine was in her bedroom, but to collect it now would mean interrupting Martha, and perhaps meeting Lyle on his way downstairs if he had delayed for a while with the children after carrying Holly to bed.

Jay lay back in her chair and closed her eyes, and allowed her mind to drift, cocooned in the warm glow from the hearth. Perhaps she dozed. Time must have passed, because when she opened her eyes again the fire had burned low. The soft glow of it outlined Lyle's figure standing on the hearthrug in front of her chair, looking down at her, the expression on his face hidden from her startled glance by the flickering shadows. An endless minute passed while he stood there and looked at her, and she back at him, time enough for her to wonder if he was really there, or if she was dreaming. Time enough for panic to return when he bent to throw another log on the lowering fire, and she realised she was wide awake, and her chance to escape the room was gone. Time enough to feel a wild, exultant joy that he had come back to her, that he had not tried to escape her company after all. She struggled upright, and he said,

'I've brought the deedbox with me. I thought it would be a useful opportunity to go through it together.'

His reason for returning was not to seek her company, as she supposed, but to work, and to ensure that she worked with him.

'You demand your pound of flesh,' she accused him bitterly, and he slanted her a sharp glance as he slid his chair closer to her own and pulled the sturdy wooden deedbox between them.

'After supper is the only time I can sit down to a job like this, and know I shan't be interrupted.'

'What about the ewe? That was an interruption.' She felt contradictory, and unrepentantly allowed it to show.

'She's had twin lambs,' Lyle replied evenly, and added, with satisfaction, 'she'll make it, the need of her babies will pull her through.'

Her own need of Lyle was more likely to destroy her, Jay thought bleakly, and stared at him uncomprehending when he added briskly,

'You have first dip.'

'Dip?' She looked at him blankly, and he made an impatient gesture towards the deedbox, and repeated,

'You have first dip from the box. I thought we'd take one paper at a time and examine it, and go through the contents of the box methodically between us.'

After a long day, he did not seem to be in the least tired, and patently he did not expect Jay to plead tiredness either. Her drowsiness vanished in a wave of indignation at his easy assumption that she would not object to spending her evening sorting his papers, but curiosity overcame her inclination to rebel as her eyes caught sight of what looked like yellowed parchment under the opened lid. Tentatively she dipped.

'It's a bill of sale of some kind.' She unrolled it carefully. 'It's dated 1511, and it's made out to a Lyall Gaunte Esquire. The spelling's different from your own name,' she observed.

'Never mind the spelling, is the document itself in good condition?' Lyle demanded, and Jay's lips thinned at his preremptory tone.

'Perfect,' she answered shortly, 'considering it's been around since 1511. Presumably the Lyall Gaunte mentioned is your ancestor?'

'He was the first owner of the Hall. The Gaunts have remained in the one place ever since.'

'How unenterprising of them,' Jay retorted waspishly, and Lyle's head came up with a jerk, and his eyes held a warning glint, but before he could reply Jay added swiftly, forestalling his retaliation, 'your dip.'

Perhaps it was the mellowing effect of the firelight. Perhaps it was because the doings recorded by the documents in the deedbox happened so long ago that they offered only a detached interest, with no feeling of personal involvement. It was impossible to argue over estate accounts four hundred years old, Jay thought with an inward smile.

'Here's a pattern of the original plaster ceiling moulds used in the dining room.' Lyle handed it across to her, and Jay took it eagerly.

'What luck!' She handled the unknown artisan's work

reverently. 'This will be absolutely invaluable as a guide when we come to restore the ceiling.'

'Here's the bill for the Van Dyck painting.'

'And here's one for the refectory table in the dining hall. Imagine, a piece of furniture of that size, costing only four shillings!'

They dipped into the box at random, exchanging their discoveries with one another, exclaiming over them like two children exploring a treasure chest, their antagonism temporarily forgotten, submerged in the interest of their search. Jay slipped to her knees beside the deedbox, and her skirt flowed out in a fan of rich colour across the hearthrug. Her face was alight with animation, lighting an answering gleam deep in the man's eyes as he watched her, but she was too absorbed to notice as the box steadily emptied, and the pile of documents grew on the coffee table beside them, until at last the bottom of the box showed that their task was done.

'At least we know the contents haven't been damaged by the fire, or by time to any great extent,' Lyle commented thankfully as together they began to replace the documents carefully, one by one, taking their time as if each was reluctant for the job to come to an end. Jay smoothed the last parchment, and Lyle closed the lid of the deedbox on the documents, and the magic moments that had passed between them, as the carriage clock on the mantel warned them melodiously of midnight.

Twelve o'clock—the witching hour. Lyle reached down his hands and caught at Jay's fingers, and she let them lie in his grasp, unresisting as he pulled her to her feet and drew her against him. The stuff of her dress settled against her slender figure with a soft sigh as she rose, as if it mourned to break the magic spell that bound her still. Slowly Lyle slid his arms right round her, but he still kept her hands imprisoned in his own, and the movement put them behind her back and arched her body against his. She tilted back her head and raised huge eyes to look up into his face, and her soft lips parted on the silent whisper of his name.

'Lyle. . . .'

Tenderly, without a trace of the harshness that rode him during the afternoon, Lyle accepted the mute invitation of her lips, and covered them with his own. For a timeless moment they clung, until Jay felt a tremor run through his body, like a spring that under pressure suddenly casts aside the control that held it tight, and vibrates with a life of its own. Without warning Lyle's hold upon her tightened, she felt the pressure of his lips increase, and the tremor gained strength and transmitted itself to her, running through her like an electric current and rousing her from the drugged sweetness of his kiss, to a pulsing awareness of the virile strength of his hard-muscled frame pressing against her, pressing her against him, stirring a wild clamour in her veins that voiced itself in a rapturous murmur,

'I love you . . . I love you. . . .'

Her lips moved under his, striving to give voice to their cry, and fell silent as they felt themselves deserted. His kiss wandered, tracing the fire-flushed outline of her cheeks, seeking the small pink tip of her ear hidden in the soft dark tendrils of her hair, and Jay quivered under his touch, and her arms rose to clasp his head and turn his lips back to her eagerly seeking mouth.

'Gaffer, can you come?'

A hard, urgent knock on the breakfast room door. The soft burr of a country voice, sounding as if it came from another world. For a brief second the firelight held them in its spell, framed in a frozen tableau.

'Gaffer?'

The voice called again, urgent, summoning. The clock struck the half hour, and the spell was broken. Lyle's arms dropped from round Jay's waist, his hands put her away from him, and he reached the door in three long strides.

'What is it?'

'It's the ewe, Gaffer.'

'I'm coming.' He turned briefly in the doorway, and his glance met Jay's across the room. 'Leave the

deedbox where it is, I'll collect it when I come back.'
Already his eyes were remote, his mind on the ewe, the
sweet, precious moments between them forgotten. 'I
may be some hours.'

He could be forever, so far as she was concerned. Jay
hated the ewe. She hated Lyle for putting her aside in
favour of the ewe. She knew she was being unreasonable,
and she did not care. She could not help her feelings,
and, she winced away from the memory, she had made
them humiliatingly plain to Lyle. That he did not share
them was equally plain, or he would not so easily set
her aside to answer the summons of his shepherd. She
burned with shame as she remembered how easily he
had tricked her into betraying her feelings, that flared in
her like the bright flame had flared from the logs in the
hearth, where now only soft grey ashes lay, telling her
the magic was gone, as surely as the bright flame was
gone from the heart of the logs, and with a bleakness in
her own heart that matched the grey of the ashes, Jay
shut the door on the room and its shadows, and crept
upstairs to bed.

The next morning Jay mounted the new lightweight
steps that Lyle had purchased for her use, and rolled
away the plastic sheet that covered the shattered stained
glass window. By doing so she made herself a target for
the cutting wind that blew unchecked through the
glassless holes, but it could not be helped, and at least
its icy bite effectively banished any last remaining
lethargy from the night before. A surge of unjustified
irritation tightened her lips as she saw that a sheet of
plywood was already securely wired to the bottom of
the steps, covering the first three. Lyle had not trusted
her to take the necessary precautions herself, and his
lack of trust rasped on her still raw nerves. Tentatively
she strode the gap to the first available foothold. Tim or
Holly would have found it impossible to reach, but she
gained it with ease, and grudgingly acknowledged that
Lyle had chosen the new steps well. They were tall, as
well as light in weight, and enabled her to reach the
highest point of the window with ease from the sturdy

platform on the top that boasted a stout grab rail reaching up above her waist, enabling her to work in complete security. It was at least as good an arrangement as her own specially made equipment, and she completed her set of measurements in record time, goaded into speedy concentration by the icy draughts that cut through her thick woolly with ease.

'Brrr! Thank goodness that part of it's finished!' She descended the steps and retreated with a shiver to the mobile gas heater, and drew out her sketching materials. She still needed the window to remain uncovered while she drafted a preliminary sketch from which she could later make a scale drawing in watercolour. In spite of the cold she worked with meticulous care. Gradually the coat of arms took shape on the paper, the shepherd's crook crossed by a sword, a mailed fist below and a fluttering banner above, surrounded by a delicate wreath of corn ears. Each detail had to be absolutely accurate, there was no room for guesswork, because it was from this that the full-sized cartoon would eventually be made in Chester, and the lovely window reborn.

'A'tchoo!'

'You're asking to catch cold by removing the plastic sheet from across the window,' Lyle remarked with asperity from just behind her, and Jay spun round and looked up into his impatient face. 'I put up the plastic cover to keep the room reasonably warm,' he reminded her unnecessarily.

'And I took it down again in order to be able to measure the window, and then make a clear sketch for my watercolour drawing,' Jay answered him flatly, resenting his implied criticism. 'I can't see detail clearly enough through a sheet of plastic to do either.'

'There's no need to complete the work in one morning,' Lyle insisted with a frown, and Jay snapped back,

'I've hardly been here for five minutes,' she exaggerated with an independent tilt of her chin. 'And I prefer to finish a sketch at one go if I possibly can.' Her icy tone matched the temperature of the wind, and asserted her right to organise her own work in the way she chose.

'You've been here a lot longer than five minutes,' Lyle promptly challenged her statement. 'It's already mid-morning.' Jay's eyes widened as a quick glance at her watch confirmed the truth of his statement. 'When you didn't appear in the kitchen for your elevenses, Martha asked me to bring your drink to you.'

A steaming mug of soup sat on the table near to Lyle's hand, and the inviting aroma of it reached Jay's nostrils as he spoke. Her interested eyes caught sight of something else beside the mug. Something large and soft, and a warm nut brown in colour.

'You need something more than soup to keep you warm,' Lyle remarked cryptically, catching her glance. 'A woolly jumper's not much use for keeping out a wind as keen as this,' he cast a disparaging look at her attire, and Jay flushed resentfully.

'I didn't come here equipped for contract work,' she reminded him sharply. 'If you remember, I came for the sole purpose of releasing two children into your care, and then straightaway to continue my journey home to Chester.' He seemed to forget she had a home, and a job, or even a will of her own, she thought angrily. 'If I'd known I was going to remain here to work, I'd have come properly equipped.'

'Since you didn't, and you haven't,' Lyle answered her evenly, 'I'll provide the equipment for you.'

'The step ladder's adequate.' She refused to admit it was ideal for the purpose. She refused to look at, let alone to mention, the plywood guard attached to the bottom.

'Let's hope you find this equally adequate, as a protection against the wind,' Lyle answered shortly. He picked up the soft nut brown bundle from the table, and shook it, and Jay gasped as a full-length sheepskin coat rolled out in front of her eyes.

'Try it on to see if it fits.' Lyle held it out towards her, but instead of turning to slip her arms into the sleeves, Jay stood irresolutely facing him, her startled eyes devouring the coat.

'I couldn't possibly work in that!' she gasped.

'Why not?' Lyle's voice was steely.

'It's . . . it's beautiful. It's much too good. It's not mine,' Jay stammered three reasons, and added impulsively, 'Who does it belong to?'

'You.'

'But I haven't . . . it doesn't. . . .' She ground to a halt as enlightenment dawned upon her. This must have been why Lyle had left her to her own devices in the store yesterday. This was why he had returned, when he thought she must be gone, to purchase the coat, probably to enlist the aid of the very assistant who had helped them in their purchase of the children's clothing. Jay's head came up with a snap.

'I couldn't possibly accept such an expensive gift,' she refused it baldly.

'Who said anything about a gift?' Lyle enquired silkily, and her face flamed. The man was impossible! she fumed angrily. To lead her into thinking the coat was a gift to her from himself, to put her in a position where she had no other choice but to refuse it, and then to totally embarrass her by denying that was his intention.

'You're impossible!' she choked.

'Regard it as workers' protective clothing,' he interrupted her smoothly, 'for use while you're at the Hall.'

'Put like that, why should I worry about the quality?' Jay shrugged, but her voice came out brittle, and her face was tense. Lyle had brought the coat down to the level of waterproofs for the shepherd, or a cowgown for the stockman, and her pride smarted under the comparison. In a tight silence she turned her back on him and held out her arms, and he slipped the coat over her shoulders. It was a perfect fit. It settled round her as if it had been tailored specially for her. The length of the sleeves and the skirt were perfect, and it was deliciously warm. The soft folds of it enveloped her in a cosy hug that laughed at the cutting wind blowing through the broken windows, and warmed away the shivers that caused her to sneeze, but it could not melt the ice in her heart that held the bleakness of an Arctic glacier at the knowledge that the warmth came only from the coat, and not from Lyle, because he had bought it merely as workers' protective clothing—her lips took on a bitter twist at the description—and not out of concern for herself as a person.

'Is it ...?' He turned her to face him, his eyes assessing the fit of the coat.

'Quite adequate,' Jay replied shortly. If Lyle expected a eulogy of gratitude for buying the coat, he was going to be disappointed, she thought hardly, and added, deliberately provocative, 'I'll return the coat and the ladder in good condition when I've finished the job here.' Lyle had brought it down to the level of protective clothing. Jay deliberately brought it further down the scale still, likening it to a mere tool for the job. 'Do you want me to sign a chitty for it?' she goaded him recklessly, wounded herself and wanting to wound in return. 'I've got some 'Equipment drawn from Stores' forms in one of the salvage boxes.'

'We'll dispense with the forms,' Lyle gritted savagely. 'This is all the signature that'll be necessary from you.'

His kiss was hard, and angry, and punished her for her base ingratitude. Jay had a brief, terrified second in which to regret taunting him and then it was too late for regrets, and the price of the coat was as nothing to the payment his lips extracted from her own, scorching them with the force of his fury, and when it was spent he thrust her away from him, white and shaking, and trembling with a cold that no sheepskin coat on earth had the power to combat.

'Drink your soup before it gets cold,' he commanded her harshly, and without a backward glance he spun on his heel and left her, and the dining hall door slammed behind him with a bang that reverberated through her taut nerves like the knell of doom. The echoes of it wakened her from her trance, and she reached mechanically for the mug of soup. It was still hot, and the grateful warmth penetrated her shock, easing the trembling, and she forced herself to drink it all before she reached once more for her sketchbook and pencil.

The soup calmed her, as well as warmed her, but it could not bring back her concentration. Footsteps sounded from outside, and she went tense, but they passed by. A closing door brought her head up, listening, but no one came. A man's voice called from the yard, and she caught her breath, but the voice belonged to the shepherd, and it called to his dog. In vain Jay tried to force her mind to pay attention to her task, but at the third false start she gave an exclamation of disgust and threw down her pencil and pad on to the table.

'This is hopeless!' she cried in exasperation. 'I'll come back later, and try again.' She picked up her empty mug and turned towards the door. She would take it back and join Martha and the children in the kitchen. Perhaps their company would restore her to normality.

'Thank you for the soup, Martha.'

'Leave the mug on the draining board, Miss Jay. Deirdre's going to do the washing up when she's finished the shelves.'

Deirdre's not inconsiderable bulk was half hidden in the kitchen cupboard, the contents of which were strewn on every available work surface within her reach.

'We're doing a bit of spring-cleaning,' Martha informed Jay with a satisfied twinkle.

'Shall I take the children out of your way?' Jay offered. A walk would do them all good, and exercise might help to settle the turmoil in her mind.

'We can't come for a walk now, Jay. There's two more lambs to feed.' Tim looked up from the hearth, his small face dismayed at the prospect of being parted from his favourite occupation.

'The children aren't in my way, just the opposite, in fact,' denied Martha emphatically. 'They're saving me the trouble of looking after the lambs. Mr Lyle brought in two more this morning. They're twins, and it's my guess they'll need a lot of help to get them on their feet.'

That meant the ewe had not made it, after all. Black depression settled on Jay, and she wished she had not succumbed to the temptation to seek company in the kitchen. In the scene of busy activity, she felt distinctly superfluous, and it was she who was in the way, not the children.

'I think I'll go for a walk.' Outside in the fresh air, she would not be in anybody's way, she thought on a wave of unaccustomed self-pity.

'It's nice enough out of doors, for all it's cold,' Martha agreed, and added with an interested glance towards Jay's coat, 'You're wrapped up warm enough for it, anyway.'

'It's a change to see the sunshine after that storm we had the other night.' Deirdre emerged from the cupboard with her face flushed from her exertions, and her hair awry, and neatly saved Jay from the necessity of explaining the coat. 'It brought down that big sycamore tree right next to my dad's greenhouse. Broke all the glass on the one side, it did.'

'Let's hope he's insured.' Jay backed out of the door making sympathetic noises, and rounded the house with purposeful steps. The felled sycamore had given her an idea.

'If we use locally quarried stone to restore the shell of the Hall, why not use locally grown oak to mend the furniture inside?' she asked herself thoughtfully. If necessary it would be worth waiting for the wood to season before use, for the satisfaction of knowing it came from locally grown timber. The fallen tree on Nathan Wilson's land might not be an oak, but it was worth investigating, and it would give a point to her walk, she decided, brightening.

It was simple enough for her to take a direction from the distant road, and Jay strode out briskly, trying not to be grateful for the perfect insulation afforded by the sheepskin coat. She fingered the lapels, feeling it safe to show her appreciation now that Lyle was not there to see. The supple leather crunched softly under her touch. It was a superb skin, made up by craftsmanship of equal quality, and at any other time Jay would have delighted in the possession of such a garment. Away from Lyle's gaze, there was no harm in her enjoying it now. She thrust her hands deep into the capacious pockets, and increased her pace as if by walking swiftly, she might leave behind the memory of how she came to be wearing it.

Black and white dots grazed peacefully at the other end of the long field, and Jay cautiously gave them a wide berth, keeping a wary eye open as she headed towards the small stand of timber two fields length away, that she remembered Lyle said housed the fallen tree. A blackthorn hedge backed by a stout post and rail fence marked the boundary of the Hall land, and Jay chose a thin spot and squeezed through, and felt thankful she was wearing her working gear of slacks, and soft-soled shoes, that enabled her to negotiate the fence with ease. She paused on the top rail. The fallen tree lay about thirty feet away. Deep hoofmarks in the still soft ground told her that cattle had been here recently, probably using the belt of trees as a shelter, but there were none in sight now, and Jay jumped to the ground. It was difficult walking across the hoof-pocked earth, and she picked her way carefully, fearful of a sprained ankle if she should catch her toe in one of the numerous hollows.

'It *is* an oak!' She forgot the cows, and the coat, and hugged herself with delight. Her intuition had paid off. The great, spreading crown of the tree had taken the brunt of the lightning flash, and there was a wealth of unspoiled timber left, sufficient to make new furniture, let alone repair the old.

'Log fires, indeed! Not if I can help it. Wait until I tell Lyle what I have in mind!' she exulted. With his deep-rooted pride in his lovely home, he could not be otherwise than delighted with such a suggestion. He was already on first-name terms with his neighbour, so negotiation for the sale of the timber should be a simple matter. The oak tree was an unexpected bonus, and Jay's spirits rose as she saw that a sheltered bank on the edge of the belt of trees had another one to offer her.

'Primroses! How lovely!' The pale knots of bloom were everywhere, forerunners of the tardy spring, and in seconds Jay was on her knees among them, filling her hands with their delicate loveliness. 'They're just what's needed to brighten up the breakfast room.' She inhaled their fresh, sweet perfume rapturously and, her posy gathered, hurried back across the fence, hardly able to wait to reach the distant buildings of the Hall.

'I'll put them in a vase and wait for Lyle to notice them,' she planned joyfully. 'That'll be two surprises I'll have in store for him at lunch time.'

CHAPTER NINE

'YOU'VE—been—*where*?' Lyle shouted.

He treated her news more as a bombshell than a surprise. Jay stared at him, aghast at his reaction when she told him the results of her morning's walk.

'You've been *where*?' His knife and fork clattered down on to his plate, and he jumped to his feet. His chair tilted ominously backwards, but he made no attempt to rescue it, and it fell to the floor with a crash. He rested his weight on balled fists on the end of ramrod-straight arms, and leaned across the table and glared at Jay. 'Have you taken leave of your senses?' he demanded.

'I went to see the tree that fell. I wanted to know if it was an oak or not.'

'You went on Nathan Wilson's land,' Lyle interrupted her accusingly, and Jay's patience snapped.

'All right, so I was trespassing. What about it?' she demanded hotly. 'It isn't such a heinous crime, after all, and I didn't do any damage. All I did was to pick a few primroses from a bank under the clump of trees on the other side of the fence. And got my shoes muddy in the process, where the cattle had churned up the field on the edge of the trees,' she remembered resentfully. Faced with Lyle's ungrateful lack of appreciation, she wished she had not bothered. She wished she had taken the primroses to her bedroom, and kept their beauty to herself.

'Eh, Miss Jay, you never did?' Martha appeared and dropped the pudding plates onto the table with an even louder clatter than Lyle's knife and fork had made. 'Not on Nathan Wilson's land?' she asked worriedly. 'Bob told me. . . .'

'What's so dreadful about Nathan Wilson?' Jay broke in. She looked from Lyle to the housekeeper in complete bewilderment. 'He can't be such an ogre, surely? He seemed civil enough when I took a message from him on the telephone this morning.'

'And remembering what that message was, you still walked on his land?' Lyle stormed at her. 'You trod under the stand of trees where his cattle habitually shelter.'

'His message said for you not to go and see him, that's all,' Jay reminded him forcibly. 'And anyway, his cattle weren't in evidence, or I shouldn't have ventured over the fence.'

'Because you did venture over the fence, it's more than likely there'll be no cattle in evidence on Millpool Hall land very shortly,' Lyle grated harshly.

'I don't understand,' Jay faltered. Her puzzled gaze took in the strained fear on Martha's homely face, the almost demonic fury on Lyle's, and an icy trickle made its way along her spine. 'I don't understand?'

'Then I'll enlighten you,' Lyle gritted, and the iron control that quietened his tone frightened Jay even more than his shout had done. 'Because of your almost unbelievable stupidity, the Millpool Hall herd might end up by having to be destroyed. A lifetime's work wrecked, for the sake of a bunch of primroses,' he finished bitterly. 'Where are your shoes?' His question was unexpected, and she stared at him, uncomprehending, and he made a gesture of angry impatience. 'The shoes you wore for your walk,' he enlarged.

'They're the ones I've got on.' She thrust her feet out from under the table for him to see. 'I wiped the mud off on the scraper outside the kitchen door.'

'I'll take them.' Before Jay realised what he was about to do, Lyle rounded the table, and bending swiftly he snatched both her shoes from off her feet.

'What on earth are you doing? Give them back to me at once!' Jay cried angrily, but Lyle ignored her as if she had not spoken, and turned to Martha.

'Where do you keep your washing soda?'

'In the scullery, Mr Lyle.' Martha evinced no surprise at the question. 'I'll get it for you,' she offered, and hurried out behind him, and without hesitation Jay jumped to her feet and followed the pair, her stockinged toes cringing at the cold of the quarry floor when she entered the scullery in their wake.

'What are you going to do with my shoes?' she demanded angrily. They were her favourite working shoes, the only ones she had with her here, and impossible to replace immediately. 'What are you going to do. . .?'

'Scrub them clean,' Lyle answered her grimly, and scooped two double handfuls of gleaming soda crystals into a bucket of what must have been near boiling water, and Jay watched appalled as he stirred the caustic solution vigorously with a boiler stick.

'You're not putting my shoes in that, they'll be ruined!' she cried shrilly as Lyle grasped a shoe in one hand, and a long-handled scrubbing brush in the other. 'Give it back to me!' she demanded furiously, and made a desperate grab to rescue her footwear.

'A pair of shoes in exchange for a herd of pedigree cattle,' Lyle gritted incomprehensibly, and dipped the scrubbing brush into the solution.

'Don't touch my shoe with that!' Outrage lent Jay extra strength, and she grabbed at the shoe and tried to wrench it from Lyle's hand. 'Drop it!' she cried furiously, and pulled at it with all her might. She forgot about the bucket. Her elbow caught against the zinc side, and the steaming liquid slopped alarmingly, and instinctively Jay loosed the shoe to grab the bucket handle, to prevent the contents from spilling over. Lyle did exactly the same, at the same moment, and released from both their grasps, the hapless shoe landed with a plop right in the middle of the caustic solution, where it promptly filled, and sank to the bottom.

'You did that on purpose!' Jay shouted at him furiously.

'For two pins I'd send the other one to follow it,' Lyle snarled back. 'At least then I'd be certain they're both thoroughly disinfected.'

'Disinfected?' The word pulled Jay to an abrupt halt. 'What do you mean, disinfected?'

'I mean that you've walked over Nathan Wilson's land in these shoes, and to make matters worse, you had to choose a place where his cattle habitually shelter.'

'But. . . .'

'I mean,' he ground on, his voice harsh and condemning, silencing her protest, 'I mean that Nathan Wilson's stockman reported one of his Herefords was blowing and off its feed this morning, which happens,' he said grimly, and his voice crackled like breaking ice, 'which happens to be an early symptom of foot and mouth disease.'

'Nathan Wilson didn't say anything to me about foot and mouth disease, when he rang this morning,' Jay denied. A shock wave of horror poleaxed her at Lyle's words, and it was all she could do to control her reaction so that Lyle should not suspect how hard his words had hit her. Foot and mouth disease. The nightmare that haunted every farmer's dreams. And she might have walked the infection right across Lyle's land, over the very field in which his pedigree herd was grazing!

'Is that you, Bob?' Boots rattled on a metal scraper, and the farmhand's amiable face appeared at the scullery door in answer to Lyle's hail. 'Where are the cattle?' he asked his man abruptly.

'Right down at the bottom end of the Long Acre, gaffer, where they've been all the morning,' Bob answered him promptly.

'They haven't moved across the field?'

'Not a step, nor they won't,' said Bob with conviction. 'There's a nice bit of young grass down there, where it's sheltered, and they're not likely to leave it until they've eaten their fill.'

'Tell the shepherd to take the electric fencing equipment, and set it up against them, to make sure they don't stray to the other end of the field,' Lyle ordered him urgently.

'I'll go and do it myself, gaffer.'

'Not now you've stepped on that boot scraper, you won't,' Lyle checked him sharply. 'Come and give your wellies a scrub in this solution before you move another step.' Briefly he outlined the reason for his command, and the consternation on Bob's honest features brought home to Jay the enormity of her transgression.

'If you wanted primroses, miss, there's enough and to spare on our own land,' the farmhand told her reproachfully.

'I didn't go out specially to look for primroses,' Jay began in mitigation, but Lyle interrupted her curtly with the question,

'Did you kneel on the bank when you picked the flowers?' Jay nodded miserably.

'Of course I did. You don't bend from the waist to pick primroses.'

'Then your slacks will need disinfecting too.'

'Surely that's going a bit too far,' Jay protested. 'You can't wash these slacks, they're made of pure wool.'

'Nothing's going too far to prevent a foot and mouth disease epidemic, and I don't care if your slacks are made of asbestos,' Lyle retorted, 'they'll be disinfected the same as your shoes.'

'I won't allow. . . .' Jay began, rebelling at his authoritarian tone.

'You will, or I'll make you,' Lyle threatened, and took a menacing step towards her that told Jay quite clearly he was in no mood to play games.

'All right, all right, I'm on my way upstairs to change.' One look at his rock-hard face convinced Jay he would not be beyond debagging her personally if she drove him to it, and it was not a risk she was prepared to take. She backed hastily out of the door, and the telephone rang as she reached the hall. She paused, and picked up the receiver automatically.

'Millpool Hall.'

'Nathan Wilson speaking.' Jay's grip on the receiver tightened until it was a wonder the handpiece did not crack under the strain.

'Yes?' Her voice came out with a croak of apprehension. What had Lyle's neighbour telephoned for? What was he going to say? Would he confirm . . .? She closed her eyes, unable to bear the possibility.

'I wanted to let Lyle know right away that he can come across to discuss the de-silting of the river, at any time he likes,' the man's voice told her cheerfully.

'Come across to see you?' Jay released her pent up breath in a gasp of sheer surprise. 'But I thought . . . you said the cow. . . .'

'Guess what was the matter with the silly animal?' its owner laughed. 'It had actually managed to eat a length of binder twine. The things animals will swallow!' he exclaimed. 'Goodness knows where it got the twine from, but it was effectively wedged, and the vet had his work cut out to remove it without choking the animal. No wonder it was blowing!'

'And is it . . .?' Jay hardly dared to ask.

'Perfectly fit now, and eating its head off to make up for lost time. Let Lyle know, will you? I wouldn't like to cause him concern unnecessarily.'

Concern was an understatement, Jay thought feelingly, but aloud she suggested, 'Let him know yourself, he'll never believe it if I tell him.' She strove to make her voice light, and her efforts must have been successful, because they were rewarded with a chuckle. Nathan Wilson thought her sally was highly amusing. Jay did not. 'I'll go and fetch Lyle to the telephone for you,' she said, and marched back to the scullery with the light of battle in her eye.

'It was a length of binder twine, not a bug, that made Nathan Wilson's cow ill,' she threw the words at Lyle without preamble the moment she entered the scullery.

'How do you know?' He looked up from the task of scrubbing her second shoe, and Jay's lips tightened ominously.

'Because he's on the telephone now, and he's just told me,' she said bluntly. 'He asked me to give you a message, but I told him to let you know himself because you wouldn't believe me.' She gave him no quarter, because he had given her none. 'He's waiting to speak to you now,' she pursued relentlessly, and with a look that told her he was still unconvinced, Lyle put down her shoe and the scrubbing brush and strode past her towards the hall.

'Are you satisfied now?' she questioned him sharply when he reappeared, waiting for the apology she felt was her due.

'Perfectly,' he answered concisely, and Jay's fury mounted at his arrogant dismissal of the subject, now he was proved to be in the wrong.

'Is that all you've got to say?' she choked disbelievingly. 'You've ruined a perfectly good pair of my shoes. . . .' She stabbed angrily with the boiler stick and fished out the sopping victim from the bottom of the bucket, and waved it, dripping accusingly, in front of his eyes.

'I've got this to say.' His face and his voice were unrelenting, denying her right to an apology, and the boiler stick wavered and dropped before the gimlet glare in his eyes. 'You took Nathan Wilson's message this morning. When you receive news of that nature I expect you to use some common sense in interpreting it.' His disparaging tone suggested that she might not possess any common sense to use, and Jay flushed angrily, but he swept on remorselessly, before she could answer, 'If foot and mouth disease *had* been confirmed. . . .'

'But it hasn't.' Jay found her voice, goaded into speech by the sheer injustice of his attitude. 'And as for using common sense, how was I to know what such a message implied? My working knowledge lies in coloured glass, not in raising cows!'

'Then it's a pity you don't broaden your horizons,' Lyle cut in grimly. 'Since you arrived at Millpool Hall you've disabled my housekeeper, and put my home, my niece, and now my herd at risk.'

'That's a wicked thing to say!' Jay flared angrily.

'It's true, nevertheless,' he insisted, and his glare challenged her to dispute the facts. 'For the rest of the time you remain here,' he commanded her forcefully, 'I'll thank you to remember that your job is to restore the place, not to destroy it.'

There it was again. The pitiless reminder, 'for the rest of the time you remain here.' It choked Jay into silence, and Lyle continued,

'It's no thanks to you that the cow had merely swallowed binder twine, and the whole thing turned out to be a false alarm.'

'What's binder twine, Uncle Lyle?' Tim trotted into the scullery and effectively put an end to the angry interchange, and Jay hurriedly grabbed the bucket and tipped the contents down the sink. If one of the children happened to get splashed with the caustic solution, no doubt Lyle would blame her for that as well, she thought bitterly.

'It's a coarse string used for tying-up jobs around the farm. Here's some,' Lyle reached up to the top of the kitchen cupboard and handed a large ball to Tim to see for himself.

'It's all hairy.' The boy fingered it curiously.

'It's rough, but it's strong. It doesn't have to look nice, like the string you use to tie parcels with,' Lyle explained, and added, 'Now I must go after Bob, or he'll be sending the shepherd on a wild goose chase to fix the electric fence at the bottom of the Long Acre, and he's got quite enough to do without wasting time on unnecessary jobs.' His glare at Jay blamed her for wasting his men's time on top of her other transgressions.

'Mind how you close the door when you go out,' Martha warned him. 'The wind's on this side of the house, and the doors bang fit to break in two every time you go through them,' she grumbled.

'The wind won't break my kite,' Tim boasted, and Jay turned to him with relief.

'Let's go out and fly your kite now, while the wind's still blowing,' she suggested craftily. She felt too churned up inside by the events of the past hour to be able to concentrate on her work, and a period out of doors with Tim and Holly might help to settle her mind.

'At least I can't fall foul of Lyle while I'm flying Tim's kite,' she told herself wryly. 'Come on, Holly.' She grasped the little girl by the hand. 'I'll help you on with your ski suit.'

'I can manage on my own,' Tim declared independently, and raced upstairs ahead of them, eager to be away.

'Don't forget your cap and gloves,' Jay called after him as, his claim proved, he emerged from the bedroom a few minutes later, suited and zipped.

'I left my kite in the kitchen.' He pulled on the woollens haphazardly and Jay released the impatient Holly to follow him.

'Go on ahead, I'll come when I've got my own coat on,' she smiled indulgently at the eager pair. She hesitated as she looked at the sheepskin coat hung on the bedroom door, then she shrugged. 'Lyle's ruined my shoes, so I might as well get some wear from his coat in compensation,' she decided hardly. Her shoes posed a problem. The only pair of lace-ups she had with her were irretrievably soaked in caustic soda. 'They'll probably have dropped to bits by tomorrow morning,' she prophesied grimly, and thrust her feet into the nearest substitute she had, a pair of low heeled court shoes. 'They're not as flat as I'd like, but they'll have to do.'

Their shortcomings became obvious the moment she joined Tim and Holly in the field outside. 'Can't you fly your kite on the lawn, it's smoother there?'

'It'll catch on the scaffolding,' Tim objected, and gave her the kite to hold. 'If you hold it up as high as you can, I'll let out the string, and you won't have to run so fast to launch it.'

She could not run at all with any degree of safety. The field was tussocky with winter grass, the earth was soft with the early rains, and her heels snagged and sank, and with no laces to hold them on her feet her shoes slipped wildly every time she tried to run.

'This is hopeless!' she gasped after the umpteenth false start ended yet again with the kite trailing forlornly along the ground instead of soaring into the air. 'I simply can't run in these shoes!' She thought of her bespoiled lace-ups, and gritted her teeth as she remembered their fate at Lyle's hands.

'I'll go and ask Bob to help us,' Tim suggested confidently.

'No, you mustn't!' Jay's voice was sharp. 'Your Uncle Lyle's angry enough with me as it is, for wasting his men's time, without you asking Bob to play with a kite during working hours.' She shivered at the prospect of Lyle's wrath if he should discover Bob indulging in such trivialities when he ought to be working.

'I know,' she had an inspiration, 'I'll stand at the top of the hill and hold the kite, and you run downhill towards the windmill, and as soon as I feel the string begin to tighten I'll throw the kite in the air as high as it will go. The wind's blowing downhill, and from that height it should get under the kite and lift it for you.'

'I'll need a good run, and Bob didn't fit a very long string.' Tim gave the length Bob had fixed to the kite a doubtful look, then he brightened. 'I'll lengthen it with a piece of of Uncle Lyle's binder twine.' He raced off towards the house, and in minutes was back again with a length of twine that made Jay amusedly afraid that his kite, if it managed to lift as far as its hopeful young owner intended, might become a danger to passing aircraft.

'Tie it tightly,' she warned, 'or you'll risk losing your kite. Don't use a granny knot, or it might slip undone.'

'I don't know how to tie anything else,' Tim complained.

'Let me tie it for you, to be on the safe side.' Jay called on her early Girl Guide training, and managed a creditable knot that was guaranteed to hold the kite firm, and handed the twine back to Tim, who rolled it tightly round his wrist.

'Wait until I get to the top of the hill before you start to run down,' Jay warned him. 'I'll gain as much height

as I can, to give the kite an extra lift.' She turned and
plodded uphill, and waved to Tim when she reached the
top. She studiously kept her face averted from the
direction of the farmyard. Lyle and Bob were working
on a perimeter fence. The sound of a mallet on wood
echoed sharply across the intervening green, and then it
stopped, and in spite of her resolution not to look, Jay
could not help turning round. Lyle's head was raised
from his task, watching her, and she tensed, waiting for
his shout.

'Surely he can't criticise us for being in this field,' she
muttered irritably. 'There's no stock in it, so we're not
disturbing anything.'

Apparently they were not disturbing Lyle, either,
because after a moment or two the sound of the mallet
began again, and Jay despised herself for the wave of
relief that passed over her, taking the tension with it.

'Now!'

Tim's shout brought her back to the task in hand.
The kite tugged in her fingers like a live thing, urging to
be free as the boy pulled at his end of the string, and
she released the kite upwards with a mighty thrust, and
watched delightedly as a gust of wind lifted it and sent
it soaring high after Tim's running figure.

'Success at last!' she exulted with Holly, and gazed
upwards entranced, lost in the half-forgotten childhood
thrill as the scarlet triangle dipped and rose at the
behest of the blustery breeze, its bright tail streaming
out behind it.

'Look, Holly, it's catching up with Tim. It's passing
him!' The breeze swung the kite faster than the boy
could run, blowing it in an arc high over his head in the
direction of the windmill.

'Let's follow.' Jay took Holly by the hand, and began to
pick her way downhill, mindful of her unsuitable shoes.

'Let's wait for Uncle Lyle.' Holly hung back.

'Uncle Lyle isn't coming, he's mending the fence,' Jay
answered thankfully.

'No, he isn't, he's running to catch up with us,' Holly
contradicted her, and Jay looked round.

'You're right,' she frowned. She was in time to see Lyle vault the fence in a mighty leap and begun to run towards them, shouting as he ran.

'Jay!' He waved his arms, and shouted again. 'Jay!' She stopped in her tracks, puzzled.

'He's waving to us to wait for him.' Holly hopped from one leg to the other gleefully. 'He's coming to play.'

'He's waving *at* us, not to us,' Jay realised with a cold feeling of dismay. 'Surely there's not a. . . .' Panic-stricken, she grabbed Holly to her, and looked frantically round for a bull, but the field was empty except for herself and the two children, and now Lyle, who gesticulated wildly as he ran.

'The kite.' The wind blew his words towards her. 'Pull in the kite!'

'Tim's only just got his kite launched,' Jay exclaimed indignantly. How typical of Lyle to be such a spoilsport, she thought furiously, to wait until the boy had been to endless trouble to get the kite in the air, and then to order them to pull it in. 'Let Tim enjoy flying his kite,' she rebelled at Lyle's high-handed spoiling of the child's game, and turned away deliberately to watch him enjoying his success. 'Why should he . . .?'

In one brief, horror-struck second, she saw why he should, and that instantly. 'Tim!' Desperately she joined in Lyle's cry. 'Tim, pull in your kite!' Stumbling in her inadequate shoes, she began to run towards the boy. 'Tim. . . .'

The child heard her call. He turned, but whether he understood her shouted instruction Jay could not tell.

'Loose the string, Tim. Loose the string!' Lyle raced past her, running flat out, and with a pounding heart Jay made what speed her court shoes allowed her in his wake. Too late she realised why Bob had attached only a comparatively short line to the kite. The much longer length which Tim had added, and which she herself tied on for him, she realised with a sob, brought the kite on level with the swiftly spinning windmill sails.

'Loose the string, Tim!' Her voice cracked with
fear, and even as she cried out she saw the tip of one
of the mill sails catch the tail of the kite and wrap
itself round the small red triangle, and the line
attached to it.

'Loose the string, boy!' Lyle roared, but Tim had the
string firmly wound round his thin wrist, and even if he
understood their shouts, he could not release himself in
time. With a shrill scream for, 'Jay!' which was to haunt
her for months to come, Tim was dragged off his feet
by the force of the mill sail's pull, and drawn by the
string attached to his wrist straight into the dark waters
of the mill pool.

'Lyle! Lyle!' Jay was not conscious of changing her
shout. She hardly realised she had shouted again. With
desperate haste she drove her trembling legs towards
the pool. One shoe stuck in the mud, and she wrenched
her foot free and ran on without it, heedless of any
damage she might do to her foot, her whole attention
concentrated on what was happening in front of her.
Numbly her eyes took in the details that refused to
register in her fear-filled mind.

A paired brace of mallard rose quacking their alarm
from the water. They flapped noisily away overhead,
leaving widening rings of disturbance on the surface of
the pool that spread to join the rings from the spot
where Tim had disappeared. Something small and
bright flashed in Lyle's hand, sunlight striking on steel,
and then he dived and disappeared as well.

'Don't hold me so tight, you're hurting!'

Holly's protest reached her through a grey mist. She
had not been conscious of holding the little girl at all,
let alone gripping her tightly. Bemusedly Jay prised her
fingers loose, and gripped them together instead,
pressing them against her mouth to force back the sobs
that she dared not allow to burst forth in front of
Holly. An aeon of time passed as she stared at the
sinister dark surface of the pool, an endless string of
terror struck seconds that seemed to go on forever, so
that an odd feeling of surprise gripped her when Lyle's

head reappeared, and then his shoulders and arms, and in his arms,

'Tim!'

A small, scarlet-clad bundle, limp and motionless. Jay staggered forward into the water to meet them. It lapped cold round her ankles, filling her other shoe, but she did not notice the cold or the wet. 'Is he . . .?' Tim stirred, and said plaintively,

'I feel sick.'

He was very sick. With deft hands Lyle turned him over, and helped him to get rid of the water he had swallowed. The paroxysm over, Tim started to cry.

'I've lost my kite,' he sobbed.

'Never mind your old kite, I'll make you another one,' Lyle promised instantly, and Jay stared at him in disbelief. In total contrast to his harsh manner towards herself, he was gentleness personified towards the two children. She felt a swift stab of envy as Lyle smiled down at the rapidly reviving boy.

'Can you stand up?'

'I think so. I'm all right now.' Tears choked Jay's throat as a ghost of Tim's customary perky grin wavered valiantly across the small, white face.

'Then run with me back to the house to get dry. It's too cold to stand about in wet clothes, in this wind.'

Remorse caught at Jay. She had been so concerned about Tim, she had forgotten that Lyle, too, was soaking wet.

'Come on, Holly, let's run behind them.'

'Don't forget your shoe.' Holly retrieved the muddy footgear, and held it up for her.

'Never mind my shoe . . . oh, all right, I'll carry it.' Jay bent swiftly and swilled it in the pool, acutely conscious that Lyle had paused and turned to watch her, his keen eyes taking in her shoeless foot, her wrecked stocking, and bedraggled other shoe.

'Come on Tim, run!'

He made no comment, he did not ask her if she could manage to reach the house without help, wearing only one shoe, and Jay felt an angry sense of rejection as he jogged away with Tim, leaving her on her own with Holly beside the pool.

'I'll have to stop for a minute, I've got a stitch.' Holly's shorter legs refused the anxious pace Jay set uphill, and reluctantly she slowed down, unable to leave the little girl on her own, and driven by her anxiety to minister to Tim.

'It's a good job these ski suits are drip-dry,' Martha's practical comment met her as she gained the kitchen at last, and asked swiftly,

'Where's Tim?'

'Mister Lyle's popped him into a hot bath, and he's having one himself,' the housekeeper answered, and her unruffled manner calmed Jay's jangled nerves as nothing else could have done. 'They'll be down in a minute for some of this hot soup. You look as if you could do with some yourself,' she eyed Jay shrewdly.

'I'll go upstairs, and help Tim to get dressed.'

'I've managed for myself.' The cause of her concern scampered into the kitchen, seemingly little the worse for his adventure, and tugged a fresh jersey down over clean trousers with an energetic disregard for the woolly that made Jay wince.

'Come and be straightened out.' She drew him to her, eager to hold him for a moment to convince herself that he was unharmed. 'Let me see your wrist, where the string was wound round it.'

'It's only grazed,' Tim held it up indifferently. 'Uncle Lyle parted the string with his knife before it had time to tighten and cut me,' he said proudly.

If Lyle had not carried the knife . . . if Lyle had not been there. . . .

'It's better not to wind string round you, ever.' Lyle *was* there, coming through the doorway and making towards the fire, talking casually as if rescuing small nephews from mill pools was just part of a normal morning's work. Jay watched him wordlessly. He had rubbed Tim's hair dry, but his own was still damp, its bright colour darkened by wet, outlining the fine, aristocratic lines of his face. Her heart gave a lurch at the sight of him, but he ignored her pleading look and lowered himself into the wheelback chair beside Tim, and took his cup of soup from Martha.

'When I make you a new kite, I'll fix a piece of wood crosswise to the end of the string, to give you something to grip,' he promised the boy. 'This way, look.' He reached for the ball of binder twine that still stood on the kitchen table, and looped a piece round his index finger to demonstrate how it would work. 'But don't tie on an extra length of string next time,' he warned seriously. 'You know, now, that it's dangerous, because of the mill sails.'

'I won't,' Tim promised ruefully. 'But Jay knows how to tie a better knot than that,' he eyed the loop of string round Lyle's finger consideringly. 'She tied the other length of string on to my kite with a knot that doesn't slip, and it held, didn't it Jay?' he appealed to her.

Jay felt Lyle stiffen. A void of silence descended upon the kitchen as Tim finished speaking. Even the clock seemed to stop ticking. Irrationally Jay strained her ears to catch the familiar tick-tock, and then Lyle brought his mug of soup down on the hearthstone with a sharp click, and the small, hard sound shattered the silence, and sent a shiver down the length of Jay's spine. Her eyes flew up to meet Lyle's, and their glances clashed across the hearth, and Jay's courage quailed at the fiery anger that glowed in his honey-gold stare.

'*You* tied the extra length of twine to Tim's kite?' he accused her furiously. 'You knew he intended to lengthen the string that Bob considered safe to fix on to the kite for him, and you allowed him to go ahead and do it? You actually encouraged him by tying the string on it yourself?'

'How was I to know the kite would blow into the sails of the windmill?' Jay sprang spiritedly to her own defence. 'How was I to know?' she demanded, with an anger that rose to match his.

'You were in the field. You saw which way the wind was blowing. It should have been a matter of simple deduction to realise the danger the mill sails presented.

Why didn't you run and pull the kite in, when you saw which way it was heading?' he demanded critically. 'You were closer to Tim than I was. You could have saved him a ducking—or worse,' he said critically.

'I couldn't run in court shoes.' Jay thrust her feet towards him accusingly. 'In case you don't remember, you ruined the only pair of flat-heeled lace-ups I've got here with me, when you soaked them in caustic soda,' she reminded him sharply. 'These court shoes are the only ones with a low heel I've got left, and it's impossible to run in them across rough, damp ground. In any case, you saw us trying to launch the kite, why didn't you do something about it yourself, then?' she questioned him hotly. 'I saw you look up and watch us, when you were mending the fence with Bob.'

'Bob assured me he'd tied a safe length of string on to the kite, so I didn't consider it necessary to intervene.'

'Jay said it'd fly higher if I had a longer string,' Tim ventured, patently puzzled by the angry interchange.

'So you not only tied the string on to the kite for him, you actually put the idea into his head!' Lyle shouted incredulously.

'I didn't know the windmill sail would wrap itself round the tail of the kite and pull it into the mechanism.'

'You should have thought!'

'And you should have thought before you left the ball of twine on the kitchen table,' furiously Jay repudiated his blame, throwing it back on to himself. 'You knew Tim was going to fly his kite, you should have known better than to leave temptation in his way.'

'When I saw the children were with you I thought they were safe. With your track record up to now I should have known better,' Lyle snarled, and Jay went white, but before she could voice the angry retort that trembled on the tip of her tongue Lyle swept on, 'Not satisfied with the damage you've already done here, you have to add Tim to the list as well!'

'Since you persist in regarding me as some kind of evil eye, then the sooner I leave Millpool Hall the better.' Jay jumped to her feet impulsively, and the sudden movement rocked her mug of soup off balance, spilling it on the table. It spread in a long stain across the white wood, dark as the anger that lay between them, but Jay ignored it. 'I'll pack my bags and go, and you can get someone else to do your restoration work for you,' she declared passionately. 'I won't remain here for another minute!'

'There isn't a train until tomorrow afternoon, Miss Jay, there's only one a day from Millford station, and it'll be gone by now.'

'Twenty-four hours will be just time enough to dry my shoes ready for packing, that is if they haven't disintegrated by now,' Jay declared viciously. 'And in the meantime,' with shaking fingers she pulled open the buttons on the sheepskin coat, and tore it from off her shoulders, 'in the meantime you can have this back!'

Convulsively she bundled the coat into a ball and threw it blindly in Lyle's direction, unable to see where it landed for the tears that flooded her streaming eyes. 'Give your protective clothing to someone else to wear!' she choked, and spinning on her heels she fled from the kitchen, running for her bedroom, and the deep soft pillow that afforded the only protection she had left to stifle the anguished sobs that bade fair to tear her slender frame in two.

CHAPTER TEN

HER lace-ups were bone dry the next morning: Moreover, Jay noticed with surprise, they had been polished. A bright shine gave the leather a look of wellbeing she had not expected to see them exhibit again.

'Mr Lyle washed them in clean soap and water last night, and then rubbed the polish well in this morning, so they shouldn't take any harm from the caustic soda,' Martha answered Jay's look of startled enquiry.

'I didn't think he'd got that much conscience,' she returned ungraciously, and bent to pick up her shoes, averting her face that still bore telltale marks of heartache and lack of sleep despite her energetic efforts with soap and water and cold cream when she rose. 'At least they're dry, and clean to pack.' Her attempt to remove the quaver from her voice was not an unqualified success, but Martha appeared not to notice anything amiss, and merely remarked chattily,

'A good log fire dries out most things overnight.' She added more fuel to its brightness from the well filled hod on the hearth, and reached up for Tim's red ski suit hanging on the overhead clothes airer. 'This is as dry as a bone, it'll be lovely and warm for him to put on to go out to play in.'

'I haven't got a kite to play with.' Its owner joined them in the kitchen in time to overhear the housekeeper's remark.

'Never mind, there are plenty of balls in the toy box, you can take a big one and have a game of football with Holly in the yard,' Martha suggested briskly, and added in a dry tone, 'You can't come to much harm in the yard.'

'Since I shan't be with them, they're unlikely to come to harm anyway.' Jay did not attempt to hide the edge

168

on her voice, and Martha glanced at her sharply, but
Tim butted in before she could reply.

'Perhaps Uncle Lyle will make my new kite this
morning.'

'He'll be too busy with the sheep, I expect,' Martha
answered. 'There've been a lot of new lambs during the
night.'

Jay felt grateful to the new lambs. She hoped they
would thrive. They had kept Lyle busy in the sheep
pens and saved her from the ordeal of meeting him at
breakfast time, and the humiliation of knowing that his
eyes would not miss the stains of tears on her cheeks,
and the dark hollows left by the wakeful hours of the
night.

'It's a ball or nothing, for this morning,' she told Tim
firmly. 'Go and sort out one from the toy box, and then
come and put on your ski suit. I'll dress Holly.' For
convenience's sake she had left the children's outdoor
clothes in the kitchen, and by the time Tim reappeared
carrying the largest ball he could find, she had Holly
zipped and buttoned, and was busily sorting thumbs
and fingers into her mittens.

'Will Uncle Lyle be able to start on my kite later
today?' Tim persisted, making short work of his own
dressing.

'Your uncle will be taking me to the station before he
does anything else,' Jay stated determinedly.

'Before I do anything else I intend to go to see
Nathan Wilson about de-silting the river,' Lyle's voice
declared, and Jay spun round, startled, forgetting her
own telltale face as her eyes flew to fix on his where he
stood framed in the doorway. He looked fine-drawn,
and his eyes were tired from his night up with the
lambing ewes, but they held a light of inflexible
determination as he added uncompromisingly, 'The
work on the river bed has been delayed for too long as
it is, to brook any more delay now.'

'You can give me a lift to the station on your way to
see Nathan Wilson.' Jay was equally determined, and
she faced him squarely across the kitchen table. Dimly

in the background she heard Martha instruct the two children,

'Run along outside, now, and play with your ball.'

She was hardly conscious of them leaving the room. She was only conscious of Lyle, and the struggle for supremacy as her will fought to gain ascendancy over his. Their glances clashed like drawn swords, and the atmosphere between them quivered with an unbearable tension as Jay girded her courage to withstand the domination of Lyle's stare.

'You can't refuse me a lift to the station.' The light of battle in her eyes dared him to refuse.

'The station's in the opposite direction to Wilson's farm,' he retorted flatly. 'With another spate of lambing due any minute now, I haven't the time to make unnecessary detours.' He refused her point blank, and Jay stared at him incredulously. A scarlet tide of wrath rushed to her cheeks like a bright banner, and angry sparks brought her eyes alive.

'Your talk with Nathan Wilson has waited so long that an extra half hour or so can't possibly make any difference,' she insisted angrily. 'And as for the ewes, I don't doubt the shepherd can manage without you for that short length of time.' The bite in her voice said she could manage without his company forever, once she had achieved her objective in gaining the station, and if she had to blink away an added brightness at the prospect, the shine of mounting fury camouflaged its real cause.

'What time do you intend to set out to see Nathan Wilson?' she wanted to know.

'Twelve o'clock.' His voice was equally curt.

'In that case, I'll be sitting in the Range Rover with my suitcase at ten minutes to twelve, waiting for you,' Jay stated imperiously. If she was actually sitting in the vehicle, he would have no option but to take her to the station, if only to be rid of her, she reasoned triumphantly.

'The train doesn't go until half past three today, Miss Jay,' Martha began concernedly.

'I'd rather wait at the station than wait here.' Vindictively Jay directed her answer at Lyle, not at the housekeeper. 'At least once I've bought my ticket I know I'll be welcome under the station roof.' She threw caution to the winds and let it be known how she regarded her position in Lyle's household.

She had gone too far. She knew it the moment she saw Lyle's face harden. A tiny pulse of fury throbbed at the point of his clenched jaw, and his eyes narrowed into an amber glare that held all the menace of a jungle cat about to spring. Jay caught her breath in a swift, indrawn hiss of apprehension.

'It's totally unnecessary,' he began angrily, when a shrill scream from the direction of the farmyard cut him short.

'Jay . . . J—a—a—y. . . .'

'It's Holly!'

Jay forgot Lyle. She forgot her packing, and her trip to the station. The unrestrained terror in the little girl's cry swept away the confused mixture of emotions that possessed her, and left only an overwhelming fear that sped her feet towards the kitchen door even before her mind had time to register what she was doing.

'I'm coming!'

Jay was quick, but Lyle reached the door a stride ahead of her. He wrenched it open and was running across the garden towards the wall that divided it from the farmyard, even before Jay was over the doorstep. With an agile bound he vaulted the wall as she ran panting to lean on the coping, and stare in horror at the sight of the two children running in full panic flight from a large, winged fury of doubtful origin but undoubted malignity, that pursued them with outstretched neck and shrill, threatening cries.

'Grab hold of her.' Lyle picked up the screaming Holly and swung her over the wall into Jay's arms, and with his own outstretched in a fair imitation of the bird he advanced upon the creature and sent it in noisy retreat towards the nearby barn.

'It tried to peck me,' Holly sobbed.

'It couldn't catch me,' Tim boasted, his courage returning rapidly now the threat of the hard yellow beak was removed.

'That brant!' Martha grumbled. 'I declare I'll have it in the pot one of these days, it's as savage as a dog!'

'It makes as good a job of guarding the yard as any dog,' Lyle remarked, and Jay's anger spilled over at his calm acceptance of the children's fright.

'Then put the creature on a lead,' she flared unreasonably. 'If you must keep a brant, whatever that is. . . .'

'A brant's a cross between a duck and a goose,' he enlightened her obligingly.

'Cross is the operative word,' Jay snapped, unappeased. 'Vicious, would be a better description of the creature! You criticised me for not looking after the children properly,' the accusation still rankled, and she used her opportunity to retaliate without mercy. 'What about yourself?' she demanded hotly. 'First Tim's nearly drowned in a mill pool that even you admit has no real use any more, and now the children can't even play in the farmyard in safety without being attacked by a creature that should either be in a pen or the cooking pot,' she agreed unforgivingly with Martha.

'If I'd known beforehand I was going to be saddled with two young children, I'd have taken suitable precautions,' Lyle growled back angrily. 'The brant can be penned until they leave, and as for the pool, that's one reason I want to see Nathan Wilson—without delay,' he emphasised, and Jay's lips tightened.

'Half an hour's delay while you run me to the station won't make all that much difference,' she insisted stubbornly. 'In any case, it's beginning to rain, so Holly and Tim will have to come indoors to play for the rest of the morning.' The warning spots settled into a steady patter, and she ushered the small pair towards the kitchen door. 'Run along inside, before you get wet.' She shooed them on their way, but risked a few more moments of rain herself to turn and throw a parting shot at Lyle.

'I'll be sitting in the Range Rover at ten minutes to twelve, ready to go to the station,' she reminded him determinedly, and spinning on her heel she hurried after the two children before he had time to reply.

She had an hour in which to finish packing. At any other time she would have organised herself in far less than an hour, but today her mind refused to function. She packed one shoe and could not find the other. She flung her clothes into her suitcase haphazardly, but where beforehand it had provided ample room, now the lid refused to shut. She gave an exasperated glance at her watch, and flew back to the kitchen to search for her other shoe.

'Don't let the children get in your way, Miss Jay. Send them downstairs to me,' Martha noted her disarray, and put it down to entirely the wrong cause.

'The children aren't with me. I thought they were with you.' Jay rescued her shoe from where it had dropped into a corner of the hearth.

'Well now, I'd better go and see where they've got to,' Martha frowned. 'They've been gone this half hour and more.'

'They're not in the nursery suite upstairs, or I'd have seen them.' Jay gave her what help she could as she made her way back to her room to pack. This time she steeled herself to fold her clothes with something approaching her customary neatness, and succeeded in shutting her case without too much of an effort. That done, she turned to the wardrobe to reach for her coat, and her lips thinned as she saw the sheepskin coat hanging beside it. Lyle must have put it there while she was out of the room.

'That's one thing I won't bother to take with me,' she muttered. She slammed the wardrobe door closed, and shut the hated coat from her sight, and groped for her suitcase with eyes that stung so that she had to fumble to find the handle.

'I don't know where those two young limbs have got to, Miss Jay. I can't find them anywhere,' Martha greeted her when she regained the kitchen.

'Don't bother to look for them on my behalf, Martha,' Jay told her hurriedly. 'I think it'd be better if I don't say goodbye to Tim and Holly, in case it upsets them.' The prospect certainly upset Jay. 'I'll put my case in the Range Rover, and come back to say goodbye to you.' She hurried out lest the wobble in her voice should become something worse, and made for the Range Rover parked in the yard.

'It's locked.'

She dropped her case on to the yard and used both hands, and tugged at the vehicle door with mounting fury, that spilled over into angry speech when it continued to resist her frantic efforts to open it.

'Of all the mean, underhand tricks to play!' Out loud she blamed Lyle bitterly for the locked door.

'I shan't be taking the vehicle out today, I've decided to go to see Nathan Wilson tomorrow instead.' Lyle's working overalls underlined his determination to remain in the vicinity of the farm, and Jay stared at him in angry disbelief.

'You've done this deliberately,' she choked. 'You purposely left the Range Rover standing there, knowing that I'd come out and find the door locked.'

'I told you I'd got no intention of making a detour to take you to the station today,' he reminded her calmly.

'And I told you I intended to catch the afternoon train.'

'I'm not stopping you,' he pointed out blandly, and in the face of his shrugging indifference something inside Jay seemed to snap.

'You . . . you . . .!' Her whole body shook with an ague of frustration and anger. 'You know I can't possibly walk all the way to the station carrying my case!' she shouted at him. It was like hammering at a rock, she told herself balefully. Once Lyle had come to a decision, nothing, absolutely nothing, made any impression upon him. His face wavered in a shifting mist in front of her eyes, and she felt a dreadful urge to pick up her case and hurl it bodily at his indifferent head, just as she had thrown the sheepskin coat at him the night before. She longed to. . . .

'Mr Lyle, do you happen to know where Tim and Holly have got to? I can't find them anywhere.' Martha's voice penetrated Jay's consciousness. The concern in it speared the mists of anger that fogged her vision, and her mind sharpened to an answering alertness as the housekeeper added worriedly, 'They've been missing for nearly an hour, now.'

'Perhaps they've gone into the barns to play,' Lyle suggested.

'No,' Martha shook her head, 'I'm sure they're still in the house somewhere. They were both too afraid of the brant to want to go outside again until you've penned it, but I've called them and called them, and I can't get an answer,' she concluded with a frown.

'They've probably found something interesting to do, and forgotten the time,' Jay put in soothingly, but Martha looked unconvinced.

'They've never missed their elevenses yet,' she answered with unarguable logic. 'And today they knew I'd made them some of their favourite gingerbread men to eat with their cocoa. I can't understand it,' she fretted.

'I'll come and help you to look for them.' Jay could not walk out, knowing the two children were missing, and there would be plenty of time afterwards for her to get to the station. 'I can resume hostilities with Lyle later,' she promised herself grimly, and leaving her case on the ground she reluctantly followed the housekeeper back into the kitchen.

She heard Lyle's footsteps behind her, but she steeled herself not to turn round. 'If Lyle searches in one direction, I'll search in the opposite one,' she promised herself, and then turned round in spite of herself as something heavy thumped on to the top of the kitchen table.

'My case?' Lyle had calmly picked up her suitcase from where she left it by the Range Rover, and carried it back into the house with him, arrogantly determined that she should not go to the station because he chose not to take her. A livid tide of colour burned in Jay's cheeks at his effrontery, and her eyes flashed fire as they met his.

'I left my case by the Range Rover ready to put it into the cab when I go to the station,' she began angrily.

'It was getting wet,' he answered with deflating reasonableness, while his tone told her clearly that he had no intention of unlocking the Range Rover door in order to put her case inside the cab to keep dry, and Jay drew in her breath with an angry hiss that rivalled that of the brant for venom.

'Eh, I wish I knew where those two young limbs have got to. Tim! Holly! Answer me this minute!' Martha padded back into the kitchen, and the worry in her face silenced the furious words that trembled on the tip of Jay's tongue. She took a deep breath, and managed in a voice that sounded almost normal,

'If they've still got their ball with them, they'll probably be in the long corridor next to the dining hall. They'll have room to roll it in there,' she suggested.

'They went that way,' Martha confirmed, 'but they left their ball in the corner. I heard Tim say something about playing a game of hide and seek.'

Hide and seek. An icy hand gripped Jay's heart at the innocent words, and the legend of the Mistletoe Bough flashed across her mind with horrifying clarity. Millpool Hall was an old house, and there were deep chests in many of the rooms, ideal hiding places for two lively children penned indoors by the weather. There was one such chest in the study, at the end of the long corridor.

'The study, quick!' She and Lyle were on the same wavelength. A quick warmth at their oneness gave her an unexpected comfort as he reached out and grasped her by the hand, and pulled her with him towards the fire-scarred room, and Jay needed no urging to accompany him. Her feet sped on wings of fear, matching his long strides, and together they burst through the study door.

'You go to the cupboard, and I'll open the chest.' He took the worst possibility upon himself, and with trembling legs Jay turned towards the big wall cupboard. The doors were stiff with long disuse, and she pulled at them ineffectually, tearing her nails, every nerve on the alert for a sound from Lyle behind her, pulling at the lid of the big oak chest.

'Please don't let him find. . . .'

'They're not here.'

A wave of faintness passed over Jay, and the room went momentarily dark. For a second or two she remained unaware that the cupboard door had swung open in her hand until a wave of dust from inside it tickled her nose, and the resulting sneeze brought back reality, and the blessed realisation that the cupboard, too, was empty.

'Nor here.'

With one accord they left the door swinging, and ran together to the dining hall.

'They've been in here.' That much was immediately evident from the wreckage of Jay's carefully executed sketch, that she had left forgotten on the long table. A scrawl that she recognised as being one of Holly's efforts to draw a picture of her teddy bear vandalised her own neatly drawn sketch and obliterated most of the carefully noted measurements, but instead of the upsurge of rage with which she would normally have reacted to such despoiling of her work, Jay could have wept with relief at the clue.

'Holly! Tim!' Immediately she raised her voice and called. 'Holly. . . .'

'Hush a minute.' Lyle grabbed her to him and put a warning finger over her lips. 'Listen!'

Jay clung to his arm, her heart thudding with a force that was almost a pain. She could feel the answering beat of Lyle's heart close against her through the blue stuff of his working overalls, and wordlessly she raised her face to his, her eyes asking a question to which she dared not give voice.

'Shhh!' He cocked his own head on one side, straining to catch a repeat of the answering thread of sound.

'J—a—a—y!'

It was so faint that, if they had been moving about the room, they could not possibly have heard it.

'Tim!' Jay's voice choked on a sob, and Lyle raised his own, strong and firm, as she faltered.

'Tim, answer me! Keep on calling.'

Tim must have heard in turn, and understood, because the faint calls redoubled, joined now by an equally faint sound of hammering.

'There's only the one cupboard in here, and we've looked in that.'

'There's the chimney,' Lyle answered her briefly. 'It's got ledges in it where they used to send the child chimney-sweeps up it.' He went down on one knee on the hearthstone and peered upwards into the black cavity. 'Tim!' A rattle of long-cold soot in the hearth was his only answer, and he swung back on to his feet. 'I can't see a thing, the chimney's blocked with generations of birds' nests. I'll have to go and get a torch.'

He was gone, and silence flooded round Jay like a threat, broken only by the faint, continuous sound of tapping.

'Tim, where are you? Answer me!' The tapping seemed to echo from every corner of the room, and Jay looked round her with desperate eyes. 'Tim!' Restlessly she prowled the room, alternately calling and listening, striving to locate the source of the tapping sound.

'Can you still hear them?' Lyle returned, bearing a serviceable looking torch.

'Yes, but the sound seems to come from everywhere at once,' Jay wailed despairingly as he made for the chimney and swung the powerful beam upwards into its blackness.

'Be careful of that burned panelling,' he warned her sharply as she turned to join him. 'You'll catch your toe on it, if you don't watch your step.'

Jay caught her toe on it, and stumbled, and to save herself she grabbed blindly at the wing of charred panelling that sagged outwards at an angle away from

the wall. The brittle remains gave way under her weight
with a loud crack, and crashed to the floor, and Jay fell
helplessly forward, her support gone.

'I told you to be careful!' Lyle dropped his torch and
caught her to him, and set her on her feet with an
impatient thump. 'Stand still for a moment while I
investigate the chimney,' he ordered her abruptly. 'I
don't want to waste time having to attend to a
casualty.'

'Lyle, look!' For once Jay was impervious to his
criticism. For once, she did not mind being accused of
carelessly wasting his time.

'What now?' His eyes were intent on searching the
chimney, impatient at being delayed by trivialities.

'Never mind the chimney.' Impatient in her turn, Jay
tugged him urgently away from the hearth. 'Look at the
wall. No, over there, where the panelling has come
away. It's Tim's scarf!' She pointed a shaking finger to
the fringe of scarlet and white wool that protruded,
unbelievably, from between two of the large blocks of
wall stone that had been hidden by the gaping wood.
'What does it mean?' she whispered. Scarves did not
protrude from the middle of solid walls. They got
caught on the top of them, or fell down by them, but
this one—she rubbed her eyes to make sure they were
not deceiving her—this one seemed to be growing out
of the mortar between the stones.

'Bless you, Jay!' To Jay's astonishment, Lyle
suddenly grabbed her, and swung her round in a dizzy
circle, and planted a jubilant kiss full on her bemused
lips, which hardly had time to register the impact before
he set her back on her feet again, gently this time. 'We
might have been hours finding Tim and Holly if you
hadn't tripped over that panelling,' he forgave her for
her clumsiness with a bear-hug that left her stammering,
and bewildered, and suddenly, unaccountably happy.

'But where ... what ...?' She let the bewilderment
come out in her voice, because she dared not let the
happiness show, in case that, too, was an illusion.

'It means those two young scamps are somewhere

behind that wall,' Lyle answered. 'If you remember, Martha said they'd gone to play hide and seek. They must have somehow squeezed into the space behind that sagging panelling, and pushed against something on the wall.' Even as he spoke his hands searched the face of the stonework, pressing against it at what he judged might be the height that Tim and Holly would press.

'Lyle, be careful!' Jay gasped. Without warning, what had appeared to be a solid block of stone began to move inwards, rotating smoothly and with hardly a sound on a central axis, but Lyle was ready for it, and remained balanced easily against its unexpected swing.

'Stand back, Tim!' he called confidently into the growing aperture, and guided the low stone doorway to a halt when it reached a central position.

'Uncle Lyle!'

'Jay!'

Two frightened, cold, and decidedly grubby children tumbled through the opening, to be scooped up into two pairs of eagerly waiting arms.

'It was cold 'n' dark in there,' Holly sobbed.

'My torch battery's run out,' Tim mourned more practically. 'And I've dented the end of it, hammering it against the wall to make you hear.'

'Never mind, I'll buy you another.' Jay felt she would cheerfully give him a hundred torches, now that he had turned up unharmed.

'How did you get in there, in the first place?' Lyle brought the emotionally charged atmosphere back to normal by demanding an explanation from his nephew.

'I hid behind the panelling, and Holly found me and tagged me, and suddenly the wall gave way and we both fell into a funny sort of room with a lot of junk in it, like an attic.'

'From the look of you, the next room you two will see is the bathroom. Eh, but you're both as grubby as chimney-sweeps!' Martha bustled in and gathered the small pair to her with a frown that deceived no one.

'We thought they actually might be up the chimney,'

Lyle confessed, 'but it seems they've found the priest's hole instead.'

'If that's what that place is, then it's high time it was blocked up. Dangerous, I call it,' Martha pronounced darkly, and shooed the children away from it like a fussed mother hen with two chicks.

'Don't go in, Lyle. It *is* dangerous, like Martha said,' Jay begged nervously as Lyle took a step inside the dark opening.

'I'll jam a chair in the door so that it can't swing shut.' He fetched one of the charred dining room chairs, and his torch at the same time. 'I want to see what sort of junk Tim was talking about,' he said, and there was an odd expression in his voice that made Jay glance at him wonderingly.

'If you go in, I'm coming with you,' she announced firmly, and taking her courage in both hands she stepped through the stone doorway after him. Coldness reached out and enveloped her, and an overpowering mustiness, born of centuries of disuse, caught at her throat as she entered the narrow, windowless room, and in spite of her resolution a small, inarticulate sound, something between fear and disgust, escaped her.

'Wait for me outside in the dining hall.' The sound was almost inaudible, but Lyle heard it, and turned instantly, his eyes alert, seeking her outline beside him in the gloom.

'No.' She shook her head adamantly, but her hand groped for his, and clung to it convulsively. 'I want to be with you.' It did not matter that he knew. She was hardly aware of what she said, only of her overriding need to be beside Lyle, even if the stone doorway closed against them, trapping them, she did not care so long as they were together. Her pride was gone, and her work no longer seemed to matter, nothing was important any more except that she must remain with Lyle. Blindly obeying her instinct, she crept close against him, too close to notice the sudden kindling that lit a glow in the warm honey-gold of his eyes as he bent his head and looked down upon her, seeking the pale outline of her face below his shoulder.

'It's dark and cold, like Holly said,' she gasped, and instantly Lyle's thumb clicked the button of his torch, and a swathe of brilliant light destroyed the darkness, and revealed in one corner the clutter of what Tim expressively described as attic junk.

'Ugh! Just look at the cobwebs,' Jay shuddered.

'Never mind the cobwebs, let's have a look at what the spiders have attached them to.' An underlying note of excitement vibrated through Lyle's voice. It reached out and gripped Jay, sweeping aside her aversion to the cobwebs, so that she craned forward as eagerly as he, and tore away the dirt-encrusted webs to reveal the now easily identifiable objects underneath.

'It looks as if someone used the place as a kitchen cupboard, and then forgot about it,' Jay exclaimed disgustedly, and her excitement died as she surveyed the heap of plates and dishes, crude double-handled drinking vessels and jars, all blackened with dirt and age, that littered the stone floor.

'On the contrary,' there was no mistaking the excitement in Lyle's voice now, and he bent to pick up a large serving dish with a reverent hand. 'It seems my ancestor used the room as a hiding place. This is the old part of the Hall,' he reminded her. 'It was occupied by my family during the period of religious persecution in the fifteen-hundreds, and what safer place to hide the family silver during the subsequent Civil War than a handy priest's hole already built into the wall?' he exulted.

'Silver?' Instantly Jay's interest revitalised, and she grabbed a smaller dish and held it up in the torch light for closer inspection. 'Of course,' she breathed, 'the blackness is tarnish as much as dirt. Think what this means?' She stared up at Lyle with shining eyes. 'If all this heap is silver, then it must be priceless. There aren't many original pieces of silver still in existence from before the Civil War. Most of the precious metals at that time were melted down to fund the fighting.'

'It seems my ancestor wasn't so patriotic as he might have been,' Lyle commented drily. 'He must have realised the danger of the Hall being occupied by troops during the fighting, and hidden all the family valuables in the priest's hole, and then panelled over the walls so that the stone doorway couldn't be discovered accidentally, like Tim and Holly discovered it today.'

'And then he died in the fighting, and took the secret of his hiding place with him.' There was a wealth of compassion in Jay's voice as she remembered Lyle's story. 'I wonder if. . . .'

They both spoke together, and then stopped, and looked at one another, and burst into excited laughter.

'The Van Dyck painting!' Lyle voiced the thought that caught at both their minds, and with one accord they translated it into action, and scrabbled among the pile of silver, regardless of the spider webs, and the clouds of dust that soon made their hands and faces as grubby as those of the two children.

'Underneath these battens of wood . . . help me to lift them. Carefully, not too fast,' he cautioned. 'If the painting is here, we don't want to damage it.'

It was in a perfect state of preservation. The rough wooden battens had protected it from the worst of the dirt, and the constant, even temperature in the small room, maintained by the immensely thick stone walls of the ancient building, had combined to preserve the paint and canvas, and the noble features of the subject, prophetically astride a charger, and with a standard-bearer in the background, gazed up at them in the torchlight as if grateful for having been released at last.

'It's the Van Dyck, there's no doubt about it.' They carried it out between them, and propped it on the table in the dining hall, and allowed the daylight to fall on the painted likeness of Lyle's ancestor. 'Look at the signature,' Lyle exclaimed, 'it's exactly like the one on the bill of sale.'

Jay ignored the signature. Her eyes devoured Lyle's face instead, trying to imprint each precious feature of it on her mind. Her own spoiled sketch, that lay beside the painting on the table, broke through the excited euphoria of their discovery, and reminded her agonisingly of the events that led up to the crisis of the children's disappearance; reminded her that, according to Lyle's reckoning, she still had time to catch the afternoon train. . . .

'What are you looking at?' Disconcertingly his eyes left the painting and fixed themselves on her.

'I . . . I. . . .' How could she tell him why she was gazing at him so earnestly?

'Tell me,' he demanded. He placed a firm hand against her back as she made to step away, and drew her back to him, and cupped the other hand under her chin, tipping her face up to meet his, forcing her to look up at him.

'Tell me.'

The excitement had left his face, too. It was replaced by a look of strange intensity that made his gold eyes glow. They burned deep down into Jay's, and in them was an expression that sent an unaccountable shyness flooding through her, a seeking that looked for something more precious than worldly treasures; a question, different from the one asked by his voice. Jay's eyes dropped, her long lashes making dark crescents on her cheeks, in which the delicate colour came and went, betraying the confusion of her mind that darted hither and thither, searching for an answer that would satisfy him, an answer that came from her mind, since she dared not voice the answer her heart would give, in case her eyes had not read the question aright.

'I was . . . I was trying to see if you resembled your ancestor,' she stammered at last, haltingly.

'And do I?' His fingers still cupped under her chin, his arm encircled her, making escape impossible, and she raised her eyes to his imploringly, silently beseeching him not to ask again.

'Do I?' he urged softly.

She did not know. She had scarcely glanced at the face on the painting. She could not see it now, because

Lyle's face was bent above her, blotting out everything else from her sight. His lips hovered palpitatingly close, blotting out her thoughts, and her own parted in a wordless murmur of longing, wrung from the rack of uncertainty that tore her heart in two. It destroyed the last bastion of her puny resistance, and a strange lethargy crept into her limbs as she yielded to the pressure of his arms.

'Lyle. . . .' She breathed his name on a long sigh, and instantly his lips crushed down upon her mouth, silencing the murmur, cutting off the sigh. The ardent pressure of his kiss sent a delirious happiness thrilling through her, telling her she had read the question aright, while it yet searched for her answer with a passionate hunger that a lifetime was not long enough to satisfy.

'I love you . . . I love you,' he groaned, and her arms rose with a new strength, the strength of confidence, to clasp his head and strain it even closer to her, lest the pressure of his lips should lessen, and the delirious happiness should fade.

'Don't leave me Jay. Don't go. I love you. I can't live without you.'

Broken, pleading words, so unlike the Lyle Grant she knew, the confident strength of the man that she had mistakenly criticised as arrogance in this, the latest scion of the Gaunt line, now pleading with her to do the one thing in the world that would give her the greatest happiness.

'Jay darling, say you'll marry me.' His lips punctuated his words with passionate entreaty. 'Tell me you love me,' he begged, and his face, so curiously like the painted face on the canvas now disregarded beside them, was taut with longing and uncertainty.

'I love you.' Her answer came low, halting, difficult to utter clearly because of the urgent demands of his lips, that clung to her own as a drowning man clings to a line that offers his only hope of life. 'I love you,' she whispered happily, and her eyes, raised shyly to his, were luminous with her love. His own fired in answer, and his arms tightened about her, crushing her to him, opening the pent-up floodgates of his love in a consuming tide of longing that for timeless minutes engulfed them both, bearing them on a crest of happiness that Jay had never dreamed would be theirs.

It spent itself, as even the fiercest tide must, and at last she laid her head back against his shoulder, with her face raised so that she could still gaze up into his.

'You're grubby,' she discovered happily.

'So are you.'

'You're tired.' The streaks of dirt could not quite erase the lines of weariness about his eyes. 'You were up all last night with the ewes.'

'I didn't have to be,' he confessed with a smile. 'The shepherd could have coped well enough on his own.'

'Then why . . .?'

'I couldn't sleep, for the thought that you wanted to leave.'

'Never . . . never. . . .' Sweetly, in the only way that would convince him, she sealed her vow to remain. 'I can wear the sheepskin coat you gave me now,' she teased him gently when he professed to believe her at last. 'You gave it to me to wear for as long as I remained at the Hall,' she reminded him wickedly.

'I meant you to wear it for always.'

'You knew, even then?' she raised startled eyes to his.

'I loved you from the moment I first set eyes on you. I was sure, on the night of the fire, when the lightning struck.'

'You let the Hall burn while you woke me up!'

'You were more precious to me than the Hall. You always will be.' Hungrily Lyle's lips traced the delicate outlines of her face, her eyes, her hair, and the blue, throbbing temples that beat only for him.

'Lightning struck twice that night,' he remembered with a tilt of his lips. 'It struck the Hall, and it struck me too.'

Lightning had struck three times, but that was Jay's own precious secret, to be told later, in his arms in the firelight, when the day was done.

'We must do something to make the priest's hole safe,' he added.

She glowed at the 'we', the precious diminutive that encompassed her whole world.

'We can bring the contents out for listing, and have the silver and the painting sent to Chester to be cleaned and restored,' she suggested, 'and then block the doorway until Tim and Holly leave.' She owed a debt to the priest's hole that would endear it to her for ever.

'We need a more permanent solution than that,' Lyle answered her gravely, and added significantly, 'For the same reason that we need to drain the mill pool.' His voice stated prosaic facts, but his look asked a question of her, and this time Jay did not hesitate to answer him. Swift colour flooded her throat and cheeks as his meaning penetrated her understanding, but bravely she met his eyes, confident in their love, confident in their shared future.

'We'll make them both safe,' she agreed firmly. 'While they're there, they'll always remain a danger to children.' Their children. Hers and Lyle's. Their own adventurous sons. A promise for the future that set his eyes afire, and brought his arms more tightly round her, his lips sealing the promise with the lifetime's security of his love.

'After the painting's been restored, it'll make a perfect wedding present for you.' Long moments passed before either of them remembered the painting.

'But, Lyle—a Van Dyck?' Her brow wrinkled. 'It's a big responsibility,' she demurred. 'I much prefer the present-day Lyle Gaunt,' she decided firmly, and Lyle laughed.

'You've already taken on a much greater responsibility,' he reminded her tenderly. 'Me, and the future of the Gaunt family line.'

Harlequin Plus

A WORD ABOUT THE AUTHOR

Sue Peters spent an idyllic childhood in the countryside of Warwickshire, England. She remembers well the primroses and violets of the spring woods, the bluebells of summer, the sweet scent of autumn's fruit harvest and the tales told by her parents in the light of cozy winter fires.

Her first taste of city life came when she went to high school in Coventry. Soon after, the Second World War broke out, and she occupied herself writing long letters to her brother, who was many miles from home. Later, on the spur of the moment, she turned a holiday adventure into an article, and its acceptance led to other articles. She also worked diligently and with pleasure as a secretary.

When her mother suggested that she should enter a fiction competition sponsored by Mills & Boon, Sue hesitated. She had never written fiction before, let alone romance fiction, but to her great surprise, her entry won second place in the regional competition—and then in the national! Encouraged by Mills & Boon, she began a novel.

Now, writing is inextricably part of her life. She says it has become a way of sharing "her" countryside with others who might one day see it and come to love it as she does.